A squalid, littered apartment . . . dusk settling on another fruitless day . . . A young man soul-weary with the tension of modern life.

A bathtub—old fashioned as one would expect to find in that dismal apartment—except that the bathtub was not there, in any apartment. It had been there—in its usual place when he stepped into it. But now he was floating in the bathtub in the midst of an endless boiling sea. In a bathtub!

One of the all time great novels of fantasy, a novel in which a modern man finds himself at odds with the Medusa of Greek mythology.

WILLIAM TENN

WORLD RENOWNED AUTHOR OF SCIENCE FANTASY

A LAMP FOR MEDUSA

DAVE VAN ARNAM

THE PLAYERS OF HELL

BELMONT BOOKS　　●　　NEW YORK CITY

A LAMP FOR MEDUSA

THE PLAYERS OF HELL

A BELMONT BOOK—June 1968

Published by
Belmont Productions, Inc.
1116 First Avenue, New York, N. Y. 10021

PRINTED IN THE UNITED STATES OF AMERICA

Contents

THE PLAYERS OF HELL

To Poke Runyon,
for old friendships.

A LAMP FOR MEDUSA

William Tenn

"And thence came the Son of Danse, flaming with courage and spirit;
Wise Athena brought him thus to the fellowship of these stalwart men.
He slew the Gorgon and winged back, bringing to the islanders
The head with its writhing snake-locks, the Terror that froze to stone."

—*Pindar, Pythian*

The bit of parchment on which the words were written in large, blotty letters had a bad smell. Like everything else in the apartment, Percy S. Yuss thought bitterly. He turned the parchment around in his fingers—annoyed at the strange discomfort he experienced in handling it—and grunted in disbelief.

Its back still had a few fine brown hairs clinging to the badly tanned surface. Someone had evidently gone to the trouble of killing an animal and skinning it, merely to write a translation of a long-dead poet's little-known verse.

Such eccentrics as these three rooms had known!

He dropped the handkerchief-size square of dead tissue on the floor, with the rest of the fantastic garbage, that varied from a ballet dancer's worn white slippers to four wooden chair legs which had evidently been chopped off with an ex-

7

ceedingly sharp axe—to judge from the unbelievable smooth-ness of the cut-away surface.

What an amazing and varied collection of junk! He shook his head as he shepherded the stuff into a great pile with the broom he'd discovered in the kitchen. A man's safety razor, a woman's curling iron, notebook upon notebook filled with strange and unrecognizable scripts. Not to mention the heap of locked suitcases on the top of which he'd just chucked his own battered valise.

In these days, one did not look gift apartments in the foyer, so to speak. Still, he couldn't help wondering why these previous tenants hadn't bothered to come back for their possessions. He found himself tingling uncomfortably as when he'd first seen the parchment.

Maybe they hadn't paid their rent. No, that couldn't be. It was such a wonderfully small rent, that even people who didn't own a half interest in a mildly bankrupt hash-house wouldn't have too much trouble raising it. It had been the lowness of the rental figure that had made Percy scramble frantically in his wallet for the thirty-five dollars' worth of cumshaw the superintendent had demanded. After years of tramping from dismal furnished room to dingy sublet to get at long last a place as cheap as this in his own name!

Percy sighed the smug, deeply happy sigh of the happy householder. It smelled, it was badly littered and would re-quire at least two full days to get clean, but it was his, all his. Enthusiastically, he bent his back into the broom again.

The hall door opened and Mrs. Danner walked in without knocking. From the living room, where he was scraping the rubbish together, Percy saw the rather badly used-up old lady who served as a combination janitor, building superintendent and renting-agent, stagger into his kitchen. A half-empty fifth of whiskey swung restlessly from one bony hand as a kind of liquid epitaph to thirty-five dollars that had once been in Per-cy's possession and was no longer.

She leaned against a wall, first patting it gently so that it wouldn't get frightened and leap away. "Good old, lovely old, moneymaking apartment," she muttered. "They come and they go, they come and they go, but you're always left for me. And every time they come, little Marybelle Danner gets

8

another ten bottles. Darling gorgeous old apartment, you're my *splurfsk!*"

The last word, Percy realized as he walked sternly into the kitchen, was not an entirely novel term of endearment coined on the spot by Mrs. Danner, as much as it was a very ordinary word dissolved beyond recognition into the hearty gulp of whiskey with which she frequently punctuated her sentences.

"Pretty apartment!" she continued, rubbing her back against the filthy wall like a kitten which had grown to lanky old age without ever having become a cat. "The owners don't pay me enough to feed the teensiest canary, my children don't care what becomes of their sweet old ma, but you watch out for me, don't you? You won't let me *sturvleglglg*. Every single time a new tenant—"

She lowered the bottle with which she had been preparing a new and moister period. She leaned forward from the hips, blinking madly through worn, red-lined eyes. "You still here?"

"Yes, I'm still here," Percy told her angrily. "After all, I just moved in this morning! What are you doing in my apartment?"

Mrs. Danner straightened. She waved her head from side to side like a bewildered grey banner. "How can he still be here?" she asked the neck of the bottle in a confidential whisper. "It's been over four hours since he took possession. None of the others ever stayed that *lurngsht*." She wiped her lips. "Not one of them!"

"Look here. I paid one month's rent in advance. I also gave you a big hunk of cash under the table, even though it's illegal. I have to work pretty hard for my money in a hot and stinking little luncheonette that seems to go further into the red with every bit of business we do."

"Too bad," Mrs. Danner told him consolingly. "We should never have elected Hoover. I voted for Al *Smiglugglug*. He wouldn't have let the Kaiser get away. Here. You need a drinkie before you disappear."

"The reason," Percy went on patiently, "that I paid you all this cabbage was so I could have an apartment of my own. I don't want you walking in without knocking. This is my place. Now was there anything you wanted?"

9

She batted her eyes mournfully at him, took another shot, belched and started for the door. "All I wanted was the apartment. But if it isn't ready yet, it just isn't *reyurmph*. I can wait another hour or two if I have to. I'm no *purksk*."

The new tenant closed the door behind her very carefully. He noticed again that there was an area of splintered wood around the place where the lock had been—as if it had been necessary to break the door down upon the last occupant.

What did that point to? Suicide, maybe. Or Mrs. Danner's mention of disappearances—could that be taken seriously? It would explain all that queer junk, all those full suitcases, as if people had just been moving in when—

When what? This was the scientific twentieth century and he was in one of the most civilized cities on the face of the Earth. People didn't just walk into a cold tenement flat on the west side and vanish. No, it wasn't logical.

Anyway, he'd better get a lock on the door before he left for work. He glanced at his watch. He had an hour and a half. Just enough time to take a quick bath, buy the lock and screw it on. He'd finish cleaning the place tomorrow.

The bath was a tiny, four-foot affair that stood high on angle-iron legs beside the kitchen sink. It had a huge enamel cover that was hinged to the wall. There was more junk piled on the cover than there had been on the floor. With a sigh, Percy began to carry the stuff into the half-clean living room.

By the time he was through, the other room was a mess again and he was hot, tired and disgusted. Trust Percy Sactrist Yuss to get this kind of bargain, he thought angrily as he wedged the cover up against the wall, filled the little bathtub with water, and began to undress. A dark, dirty apartment, filled with the garbage of countless previous tenants, and not only had he had to pay extra money to get the place, but now it seemed there was a curse on it too. And a curious drunken female superintendent who would probably let him have all the privacy of a hot suspect in the Monday morning police line-up!

He took a towel and a fresh bar of soap from his valise. His mood grew blacker as he realized his feet had become coated with a kind of greasy grime as a result of standing on the kitchen floor. The place probably had vermin, too.

Bending down to brush off his feet so that he wouldn't carry the soil requirements of a potato patch into the bathtub, he noticed a scrap of white on the floor. It was the parchment with the fragment of classic poetry laboriously traced out on one side. He'd scuffed it into the kitchen while tramping back and forth.

As he glanced at it cursorily once more, another peculiar electric shiver went through him with the force of a galloping virus infection:

". . . He slew the Gorgon and winged back, bringing to the islanders
The head with its writhing snake-locks, the Terror that froze to stone."

Who was it who had slain the Gorgon? Some character in Greek mythology—but who exactly he just couldn't remember. For some reason, the identity and the name escaped him completely. And usually he had a fine memory for such little items. Twenty years spent working out crossword puzzles after a frenzied day dealing them off the arm in dining-cars was almost the equivalent of a college education.

He shrugged and flipped the parchment away. To his annoyance, it bounced off the upright bathtub cover and into the water. Trust his luck! He hung the towel on a crossbar of the tall bathtub legs and climbed in, having to duck his head and twist his shoulders down laboriously to avoid the wooden dish-closets set on the wall some three feet above the tub.

His knees were well out of the water in the little bathtub, practically digging into his chest. Washing himself under these conditions was going to be real cozy!

It was impossible now to recapture the earlier mood of exultation at having an apartment of his own. He felt he'd been taken, as he'd felt all through his life after being persuaded to go into some scheme or other. Like buying a half-interest in a restaurant which the sheriff already regarded with fond proprietary interest.

"I'm not even taken," he said unhappily. "I give myself away!"

And on top of everything, the plug leaked! The level of water sank rapidly down to his hips. Cursing his parents for being attracted to each other in the first place, Percy reached

11

forward to jab it more securely in place. As he did so, the parchment, floating face up on the water, caught his eye.

Long strands of hair now trailed it wetly, and the words were beginning to dissolve in the water. He wasn't interested in it; more, he felt very strongly that he shouldn't be interested in it, that here, in this bit of archaic verse, was more living danger than he had ever known in his screamingest nightmares. He felt that strange tingle begin again in the inner recesses of his body, and he knew that his instincts to toss it away had been right, that the curiosity that impelled him to read it every time he picked it up was utterly, terribly—

"And thence came the son of Danae—"

Almost against his will, his mind wondered. *Thence?* Where *thence?* Somehow, he felt he knew. But why should he feel that way? He'd never read a line by Pindar before. And why should he be wondering about it in the first place? He had other troubles, lots of them.

His hand swept the parchment up like a particularly disgusting insect. Up and over the side of the bathtub. Right into the bluish waves that billowed all around him.

Into the sea.

He hardly had time to let his jaw drop. Because the bathtub began to sink. Percy was bailing before he realized he was doing it.

This time the water was bubbling into the tub. With a convulsive gesture of his entire body that almost threw him over the side, he clamped his left foot down hard upon the defective plug and splashed the tepid mixture out with two threshing, barely-cupped hands.

In spite of his inaccurate roiling and tossing, he had the tub all but emptied in a matter of seconds. A thin trickle of sea-water still lounged out from between his toes. He reached over the side, noticing uncomfortably that the rim was a bare two inches above the sea's restless surface. Yes, the towel was still in place, knotted intricately around the cross-bar. It was soaking wet, but it made a magnificent reinforcement for the plug. With fingers that had sharpened into a remarkable deftness under the grinding surprise of the moment, he jabbed corners of the towel all around the edges of the rubber plug.

Not perfect, but it would hold back the waters. Now, where was he?

He was in a bathtub which—temporarily at least—was floating in a warm and only slightly choppy sea, a sea of the deepest, most thrilling azure he had ever seen. Ahead, an island rose in a mass of incredibly stately and delicately colored hills.

Behind him there was another strip of land, but it was lost in a gentle mist and was too far away for him to determine whether it was an island or the outstretched finger of a continent.

To the right, there was more blue sea. To the left—

Again he almost fell out of the tub. Some fifty feet off to the left was quite the largest sea-serpent he had ever seen in or out of the Sunday Supplements.

And it was humping along the waves directly at him!

Percy leaned forward and paddled madly at the water on both sides of his tub. What a world, he thought, what an insane world for a quiet man to find himself in! What had he ever done to deserve—

He heard a peculiar rattle of sound, like a cement-mixer gargling, and looked up to see the monster staring down at him through unwinking eyes. It was, the back of his mind gibbered, all of two feet in diameter: no doubt it could swallow him without even gulping. A row of bright red feathers plumed up from the top of his head as the great mouth opened slowly to reveal countless rows of jagged, fearful teeth.

If only he had a weapon! A knife of any sort, a stone, a club . . . Percy clambered upright in the tub, his fists clenched desperately. As the mouth opened to its fullest width and the forked tongue that looked as sharp and deadly as a two-headed spear coiled back upon itself, he lashed out with his right arm, putting into the blow all the strength of cornered despair.

His fist caught the beast on its green lower lip.

"Ouch!" it said. "Don't do that!"

It swirled away from him so vehemently that his little enameled craft was almost swamped. Licking its lip with its

13

flickering tongue, it paused to stare back at him indignantly over a glistening coil.

"That hurt, you know! All I wanted to do was say, 'Welcome, son of Danae,' and you have to go and bop me one! You won't make many friends acting like that, I can tell you!"

The monster swam a bit further away and curved to face the goggling Percy standing limply in his bathtub.

"You didn't even ask if I was working for the snake-mother or Poseidon or whatever! Maybe for all you know I'm an independent operator. Maybe I have a bit of information that would save your life or the life of someone pretty important to you. No, all you can do is hit me," the creature sneered. "And on the lip, which as everyone knows is my most sensitive part! All right, son of Danae, if that's the way you want it, that's the way it's going to be. I won't help you."

With a kind of rippling shrug that threaded disdainfully from the enormous head down to the thin delicacy of a tail, the sea-serpent dived. And was gone.

Percy sat down carefully, feeling the hard sides of the tub as caressingly as if they were his own sanity.

Where in the world was he? Or, rather, where out of it was he? A man starts to take a bath in his new apartment and winds up in——in—— Was that how the others had gone?

He stared over the side through the clear sea. The legs of painted angle-iron which had supported the bath-tub were sheared off cleanly about halfway down. Fortunately, the faucets had been shut off; the pipes were also cut. Like something else. He remembered the chair legs back in the apartment.

Four chair legs minus a chair. Somewhere, then, in this world there might be a chair without legs. Containing someone who had purchased an apartment from Mrs. Danner.

Percy realized suddenly that there was a very bad taste in his mouth. An awful taste, in fact.

Of course. The soap. When he'd started bailing upon arrival in this weird place, he had a cake of soap in his hand. He'd stuck it in his mouth. And up to now he hadn't had a really peaceful moment in which to remove it.

He extracted the somewhat soggy pink bar from his teeth

14

with a distinct lack of relish and washed his mouth out carefully with sea water. As he did so, he noticed that he had drifted much closer to the island. There was evidence of life somewhere behind the beach, a few slowly moving human beings and a cluster of huts or houses—at this distance it was hard to tell which.

What were his resources in dealing with this new world? He considered them ruefully. A slightly used cake of soap. An extremely wet bath towel. A round rubber plug, too badly worn to do its job properly. And a bathtub, if he could move it once he got to shore.

Then, of course, there was himself. "Like if the natives go in for human steak," he grimaced.

A sea-serpent that talked! Whose dignity had been injured, who had even gone so far as to— Wait a minute! What had it called him?

Son of Danae.

But he wasn't!

"Go tell the sea-serpent," he told himself fiercely. He remembered the verse on the bit of parchment abruptly: *"The head with its writhing snake-locks—"*

"I've got to get out of here!" he commented restlessly and with tremendous conviction, glancing from the rocking tub to the placid rolling sea from which anything might be expected.

For a moment, when the net flapped down upon his shoulders, Percy had the frantic idea that he'd been overheard by some deity who had hurried to cooperate. He struggled, threshing wildly against the coarse, knotted fibers that tore at his skin. Then, as he felt the entire tub caught in the huge skein and being drawn rapidly toward shore, he relaxed into *now what?* hopelessness and tried to see what had happened.

He had drifted in front of a cliff-like promontory of the island. A group of men dressed in loincloths were dancing about on the edge of the cliff, cheering a richly-clad fellow who, from a precarious foothold halfway down the steep face, had flung the net and, with dexterous twists of wrist and forearm, was now hauling it in.

"Attaboy, Dictys!" one of them yelled as the tub beached, turned over and, with Percy crashing around under it, was dragged up the side of the cliff. "You got it all right, all right."

"That Dictys," another commented admiringly. "He's death on sea monsters. This'll be the third he caught this week."

"The fourth," Dictys corrected as he scrambled to the top of the cliff with the bathtub and the net-enclosed man both securely on his shoulder. "You forgot the pigmy mermaid—half-woman, half-sardine. I count it even though she was kind of small. But this'll be the best of the lot. I've never seen anything like it before."

He unwound the net rapidly with long-practised gestures. Percy climbed out of the tub and flopped on the ground. He felt like a bag of well-gnawed bones.

Dictys picked him up with a huge hand, held him out for inspection. "This isn't a monster," he said in evident bitter disappointment. "It comes apart: half of it is a man and the rest is a round sort of chest. And I thought it was something really unusual! Oh well," he mused, lifting Percy over his head with the obvious intention of throwing him back into the sea, "You can't hit it all the time."

"Maybe," suggested an oldster on the edge of the group, "maybe he is a monster. He could have changed into a man just now. He might know that if he's a monster we'd put him in your brother's zoo, but if he's a man we'd throw him back because we've got lots of people here already."

The tall man nodded thoughtfully. "You might have something there, Agesilaus. I'd hate to go back to King Polydectes empty-handed. Well, there's an easy way of finding out."

What kind of world is this? Percy was frantic "—if he's a man we'd throw him back because we've got lots of people here already!"

And what kind of test were they going to apply?

He noticed that the well-dressed fisherman had unsheathed the great single-bladed sword he wore on his back. He ground the point of it into Percy's chest interrogatively.

"You better change to your particular monstrous form fast, sonny. Because you're not going to have the pleasure of being returned to the drink. Instead, I'm going to cut you up into six distinct and separate slices in just a few seconds.

16

You'll be *much* better off in my brother's cages. Now then, what exactly are you?"

Percy beat against his forehead with an open palm. What was he supposed to do—develop a quick-change routine on the spot that included wings, flippers and a Siamese twin? Because if he didn't, he was evidently going to become cutlets.

"All right," Dictys said, frowning. "Go ahead—be stubborn. See what it gets you."

He whirled the bronze blade experimentally around his head, then curved it back for a tremendous stroke.

Percy swallowed as he saw it glint redly at him. "I'll talk," he babbled. "I'll tell you about myself! I'm—I'm—"

What could he tell them that would make sense in their terms? What kind of lie could he compose in a hurry that they would believe? They wanted him to make like a monster.

Monster! He'd talked to a—

The words boiled rapidly out of his lips. He had no time to weigh them. "I'm the man the sea-serpent welcomed as the son of Danae." He hoped it would at least give the big fellow pause.

It did.

Dictys lowered his sword and stepped back staring. "The —the son of Danae? The one who's going to kill the Gorgon?"

"The same." Percy nodded with the self-conscious grandeur of a celebrity discovered by the night-club m.c. at a ringside table. "The . . . the famous Gorgon killer. The—the man who brought the islanders the head with the writhing snake-locks, the Terror that—"

"Who *will* bring, you mean," Dictys corrected him. "It's not done yet. Well, well, well. You're kind of scrawny for that sort of job, even if you do have red hair. What's your name?"

"Percy. Percy S. Yuss."

"Right!" Agesilaus yelped from the rear. He came hurrying up, his beard flaunting behind him like an oversized white woolen necktie. "It figures, Dictys, it figures! Right on the dot of the prophecy. His name's Perseus, he has red hair, you

17

caught him in a fishnet—everything happened exactly the way the oracle said—"

Dictys thrust out his lower lip and shook his head. "Oracles are one thing. Muscles are another. Nobody's going to tell me that this weakling is going to tackle the beast that frightens the bravest men and even other monsters, no matter how powerful. Look at him—he's quivering with fear already!"

This was not exactly true. Percy became chilled standing on the windy hillside in nothing but his wet skin. There was, besides, an emotional reaction to all his recent experiences setting in. But there was also a mounting discomfort at the way they were discussing his capabilities as a Gorgon-killer. He'd thrown in the sentence merely as a means of distracting Dictys temporarily; now it seemed they couldn't get off the subject. The beast that frightened men and gods!

He thought back wistfully to a few minutes ago when he'd been riding a serpent-infested sea in a leaky bathtub. Ah, those were carefree, happy times!

"His name's not even Perseus," Dictys was arguing. "It's Persaesus or something. You're not going to tell me that this bedraggled bumpkin will become the most famous hero of all time?"

Agesilaus nodded vehemently. "He certainly will! As far as the name's concerned, I think it's close enough. Sometimes the oracle gets names mixed up. But here's the chest in which the oracle said Perseus would arrive with his mother, Danae, after King Acrisus of Argos tossed them into the sea."

"Yes, but the oracle said the infant Perseus," another loinclothed man broke in. "Didn't she?"

"Well," Agesilaus hedged. "Sometimes the oracle gets ages mixed up too." The old man looked a little now as if he were no longer certain about oracular dependability on any matter.

Percy found himself sympathizing with him. Agesilaus was evidently pleading his case, but he wasn't certain which way he'd be worse off, if the old man won or lost.

Dictys came in fast for the argumentative kill. "If King Acrisus of Argos, according to the oracle, threw Perseus and his mother into the chest, then where is Danae? And another thing, Agesilaus. Argos is that way," he pointed with a brace-

18

leted hand. "Northwest. This fellow came from the east. No, he's an impostor trying to cash in on the prophecy. And I don't like impostors."

He reached down for a couple of lengths of rope with which several of the men had been repairing holes in the net. Before Percy could get a word of protest out of his slowly opening mouth, he was tripped expertly and tossed to the ground. In a moment, he was tied up as tightly as an expensive Christmas present.

"What's the penalty for impersonating a hero?" Dictys asked Agesilaus. The packaging job completed, he removed his knee from the gasping young man's back and rose.

"For impersonating a hero," the old man said thoughtfully, with an unsatisfied frown still creasing his face, "the penalty's the same as for blasphemy. Cooking over a slow fire. In fact, since your brother, King Polydectes, reformed the legal system, practically every crime is punishable by cooking over a slow fire. Your brother says it makes it easier for him to pass sentence that way. He doesn't have to remember a whole calendar of complicated punishments."

"That's why we call him Wise King Polydectes," one of the younger men exclaimed, and everyone nodded enthusiastically.

"Listen—" Percy began screaming from the ground. Dictys stuck a handful of grass into his mouth. There was enough loose soil attached to make the gag a verb as well as a noun. He was so busy strangling that he had little energy for observation and less for an attempt to escape when two of the men slung him to a pole and began carrying him downhill over highly uneven ground.

"Hi, there, Menon," he heard someone call as he was borne choking and sneezing along a dusty road. "Whatcha got?"

"Don't know for sure," the forward bearer replied. "I think it's kettle bait."

"You don't say! This crime-wave gets more frightening every week!"

By the time Percy had worked the last of the foliage out of his mouth, they had passed through the huge gateway of a

19

stone-walled citadel and into a cluster of small but surprisingly well-built brick houses.

His pole was placed in two forked sticks set upright in the main thoroughfare of the town. He dangled from the tight ropes, feeling his blood grinding to a halt.

A group of curious men and women gathered around asking questions of his two guards.

"Is that the latest monster Dictys has caught?" a woman wanted to know. "He doesn't seem to be very unusual." She poked experimentally at choice spots on his naked body. "Practically normal, I'd say."

"Stew-job," the bearer said laconically. "Nice tender stew-job."

As far as was possible in his tightly laced condition, Percy writhed. No, this couldn't be happening to him—this just couldn't be! A man doesn't start taking a bath in a new apartment and wind up in a world where everything from burglary to barratry is punished by—

"I will not consider that thought," his mind announced. "I know when I'm well off."

Certain things were clear to him, though, disagreeably clear. He had somehow fallen into a past which had never really existed, the time of the Greek mythos. Never really existed? The sea-serpent's indignation had been real enough, and so were the ropes with which he was bound. So, he suspected, would be the punishment, if he were found guilty of impersonating a hero.

Odd, that. The serpent addressing him as the son of Danae, who was evidently the mother of Perseus. His own name, which formed a combination of syllables remarkably like the Gorgon killer's. The bit of parchment he'd found in the apartment which evidently had helped precipitate him into this mess, and the subject of the snatch of poetry written upon it. The way he'd come close to the legend in various other ways, such as the arrival by sea—

No! When his trial came up, he wanted to plead absolute innocence, that he had no knowledge whatever of the Perseus prophecy and no interest at all in it. Otherwise, thinking all those other thoughts could only lead in one direction. . . .

He shivered violently and vibrated the pole briefly.

"Poor fellow, he's cold!" a girl's voice said sympathetically.

"That's all right. King Polydectes will warm him up," a man told her. Everyone guffawed. Percy vibrated the pole again.

"I never said I was Perseus!" the bound young man broke out despairingly. "All I did was tell your Dictys that the sea-serpent—"

"You'd better shut up," the bearer who had been called Menon advised him in a confidential, friendly manner. "For trying to influence the jury before a trial, you can have your tongue torn out by the roots—whether you're eventually found guilty or innocent."

Percy decided to keep quiet.

Every time he opened his mouth, he put the local criminal code in it. He was getting deeper and deeper into the most fantastic trouble and didn't have the slightest idea how to go about getting out of it. Or how he'd gotten into it in the first place.

Mrs. Danner. He hated Mrs. Danner, how he hated that profiteering old female souse! She, if anyone, was responsible for his present situation. She'd evidently known that the apartment was some kind of exit apparatus; when she'd walked in unannounced, she had expected to find the place empty. If only he'd given a little more attention to her gleeful maunderings!

How long had people been noticing that sign outside the tenement entrance? "Three-Room Apartment for Rent. Very Cheap. Immediate Occupancy!"

How many had run in and excitedly paid her the thirty-five dollars "renting-fee" she demanded, then bolted home to gather up enough personal belongings to take formal possession? And then, a few moments after entry, while measuring the bedroom for furniture arrangements perhaps, or considering the walls relative to a daring color scheme idea, or prying loose a badly stuck window—had suddenly fallen through into this world of magic and violence?

How long had Mrs. Danner been making a good thing out of this apartment, how many "renting-fees" had she acquired? Percy didn't know, but he thought dreamily of coming upon her some time in a locked room. Forgetting his painfully bound hands and feet for a moment, he mused

21

gently on the delightful softness of her throat under a pair of insistent thumbs.

Although she couldn't be the whole answer. She didn't know enough about anything outside of the latest quotations on whiskey-by-the-case-F.O.B.-distillery to have created the peculiar chronological trap that the apartment contained. Who was it then? Or what? And, above all and most important, why?

Dictys had come up, surrounded by his bully-boys in semi-sarongs.

"A bad day," he told the townsfolk. "Didn't catch a single solitary horror. Just this fake hero."

"That's all right, Dictys," the man who had previously expressed confidence in the King's thermal reliability reassured him. "He'll still be a good excuse for a party."

"Sure," someone else chimed in. "With an execution, the evening won't be entirely lost."

"I know, I know," Dictys admitted morosely. "But I wanted a specimen for the zoo. An execution won't be the same thing at all."

While most of the surrounding individuals applauded the extremely commendable detachment of so scientific an attitude, Percy saw a man with a voluminous white mantle push out to the front of the group and look at him more closely and curiously than anyone else had. The man had a peculiarly bright saffron skin, Percy noticed, when a fold of the cloak came down from his face for a moment.

"What made you think he was a monster?" the man asked Dictys, putting the fold carefully back in place.

"The chest he was riding from the cliff, it looked like part of him. It was round and white and had all kinds of metal pieces sticking out. I've never seen anything like it before—and I've been to the mainland twice."

"Where is the chest?"

The large man pointed over his shoulder with a thumb the size of a small banana. "Oh, we left it on the cliff with the rest of the stuff he had in it. You can never tell about strange pieces of furniture: sometimes they come alive or burst into flame or— Say! Are you a stranger in town?"

The white-cloaked man dropped a hand to his mid-section.

22

He passed it once across his abdomen and, as Dictys advanced truculently upon him, he disappeared.

There were breaking bubbles of comment all through the crowd.

"What was that?"

"Where in the world did he go, Eunapius?"

"I don't know but, if you ask me, he wasn't all human."

"Mama, I wanna go home!"

"Sh-h-h, Leontis. There may be a cooking today. You wouldn't want to miss that, would you?"

"What do you think he was, Dictys?"

Their leader scratched his matted hair. "Well, he couldn't have been what I thought he was, just an ordinary stranger passing through. I wanted to grab him and put him under arrest. If he was a stranger or a wandering merchant and had forgotten to register with the commander of the palace guard, he'd have been liable to the Foreigner's Penalty Tax."

"You mean all his goods impounded and his right arm burned off before his face?"

"More or less, at the discretion of the guard commander. But I think he must have been either a wizard or a major monster. In fact, from the color of his skin, I'd say he was a human-type monster. Wasn't it gold?"

Agesilaus nodded. "It was gold, all right. What they call on the mainland the *Olympian* type of monster. Those aren't supposed to be too bad. According to the mainlanders, they help men lots of times."

"When they help men, it's for their own good reasons," Dictys growled. "Not that I have anything against major monsters," he explained hurriedly to Agesilaus. "They have their own private quarrels and men should stay out of them if they don't want to get badly hurt."

From the anxious speed with which he had added the last remark, Percy deduced a certain real fear of what the man called "major monsters". Evidently, minor monsters were something else again, since Dictys had been fishing for them and the king maintained a kind of zoo. But why had the golden-skinned stranger been so interested in him? Had he something to do with Percy's arrival here?

He had long lost all feeling in his wrists and ankles and

23

was wondering dizzily if they intended to keep him hanging in the village square as a kind of permanent decoration, when there was a musical clank of metal armor and an uneven tramping of feet.

A very hoarse voice said, "King Polydectes of Seriphos will see the prisoner now."

Percy sighed with real gusto as two men shouldered his pole again and began jouncing him along the main avenue. Not only was he going to go to a place where his side of the story could be heard at last, but he now knew the name of the island kingdom on which his errant bathtub had stumbled so unceremoniously.

Seriphos. He went through his memory rapidly. No, he didn't know anything about an island called Seriphos. Except what he had learned in the past hour or so. That it was fairly close to the Greek mainland and therefore in the warm Aegean Sea. And that it was awaiting the fulfillment of an ancient legend to the effect that the Gorgon-killer Perseus was to land there sometime before starting out on his heroic quest.

Also, that it had a judicial system that bore a close resemblance to a power saw.

He was carried up a single step and into a courtyard with an enormous ceiling supported by four massive pillars of stone. Menon slipped the pole out of the rope loops at his hands and feet, and the other bearer cut his bonds with a few generous slashes of a long bronze knife.

They stood him on his feet and stepped back. "Feel better now?"

Percy pitched forward on his face. He bounced hard on the painted cement floor.

"His legs," Menon explained to his buddy. "They've fallen asleep."

"Always happens," the other said professionally. "Every damn time."

The return of circulation was grim, swirling agony. Percy moaned and rolled about on the floor rubbing his wrists and ankles with hands that felt like wooden boards. A few people came over and squatted down beside him for a moment to stare at his face or watch his struggles. No one offered to help.

24

After a while, he was able to bow-leg painfully upright. His guards grabbed him and shoved him between them against a pillar.

Most of the townspeople had followed him into the hall. The news was spreading, it would seem. Every few moments someone else came in—butchers with their dripping meat cleavers, peasants with their scythes, women carrying rush baskets filled with berries and vegetables.

The newcomers would have him pointed out to them. Then they would either smile and nod slowly in satisfaction, or they would turn and run out fast, in evident haste to get Cousin Hybrias or Aunt Thea before all the fun was over.

In the middle of the courtyard, beside a blackened hearth roughly the size of the entire apartment which Percy had so recently vacated, a man sat on an enormously wide stone throne.

At first glance, he seemed to be lolling in a large number of strangely shaped cushions. Closer examination, however, revealed the cushions to be a fine collection of young and pretty girls who varied as much in their coloring as they did in their interest in the affairs of state going on before them. One extremely pretty blonde who formed part of the king's foot-stool was snoringly sound asleep. Another, a gorgeous Negro girl, most of whose body was obscured by a large masculine shoulder, was expostulating vehemently into the monarch's right ear and waving her hand at a moaning figure prostrate before the throne.

"See here, Tontibbi," the king told her at last in a highly exasperated voice, "I've got my own system of punishments and I don't want any decadent females from an over-civilized part of the world to be suggesting changes all the time no matter how imaginative they might be. We're rough-and-ready folk here on Seriphos, and we go in for simple entertainments. And if you African snobs want to go around calling us barbarians, well go right ahead. We're proud of the name."

The dark girl scowled and subsided back into the recesses of the great throne. The assembled crowd applauded vehemently.

"That's the way, Polydectes. You tell these stuck-up foreigners where to get off!" an elderly farmer cheered.

25

"Well," Polydectes said slowly and thoughtfully. "The way I see it—why shouldn't what was good enough in my father's day be good enough for me?"

"Don't you just love the way he puts things?" a beaming housewife remarked to her neighbor. "I think it's lovely to have a king who's so clever with words!"

"Besides," her friend replied, "I don't understand all this crazy desire for change all the time. What could be better than disposing of criminals by cooking them over a slow fire? The way King Polydectes' chef does it, we usually get four or five hours out of the weakest man. He starts after supper and by the time he's through it's quite dark and everyone feels like having a good night's sleep after a fine, enjoyable evening. Personally, I wouldn't dream of asking for anything more."

Percy felt his stomach turn in a slow, rocking half-circle. The man who was lying before the king screamed a little bit and tried to grind his face into the cement floor.

What kind of people were they anyway? They talked of the most horrible things with the same equanimity as if they might be discussing the latest movie or wrestling match they'd seen the night before on television.

Well, of course, public executions were the closest these people came to such things as movies or television. Percy remembered stories he'd read in the newspapers of crowds turning out to attend hangings in various parts of the United States. That was the twentieth century! And an execution was still a sufficiently fine spectacle for many men to bring their dates, for some women to bring their children and for a few enterprising businessmen to hawk tiny replicas of the gallows on which a fellow-human was frantically kicking his life away.

All of which was well and good, but didn't help him very much in his present predicament. If only he could figure out some approach which these people would honor, if only he could learn a little bit about their ideas of right and wrong in time to do himself some good!

He strained to catch every detail of what was going on. He needed clues as to their courtroom procedure. Would he get a lawyer to defend him? He doubted it from what he'd seen so far. Yet there had been talk of a trial, there had been mention of a jury. There was a little frozen comfort in these civilized institutions no matter how they were applied, he decided.

And then he wasn't so sure.

"I'm getting tired of this," the king broke into the prostrate prisoner's broken-hearted babble. He lifted his head and waved vaguely at the assembled crowd. "Hey, jury! Any of you willing to insist on this man's innocence?"

"Uh-uh. Guilty!"

"Guilty as hell!"

"The low-down beast! Cooking's too good for him. Hey, Brion, what'd he do?"

"How should I know? I just came in. Must have been something bad or he wouldn't be on trial."

"Guilty, guilty, guilty! Let's get on to the next case. That looks good!"

"Raise the prisoner for sentencing," King Polydectes commanded. Two guards leaped forward and lifted the writhing, pleading man. The king pointed a forefinger solemnly at the ceiling. "By virtue of the power vested in me by me," he intoned, "I hereby sentence you to—to . . . just a minute now. To—"

"To cooking over a slow fire," the Negro girl behind him said bitterly. "Is it ever anything else?"

Polydectes pounded a barrel-like fist angrily into his open palm. "You better be careful, Tontibbi! You'll go into the kettle yourself if you don't watch out! You might have spoiled the whole legality of the trial! All right, take him away," he said in disgust. "You heard what she said. Do it."

"I'm sorry, Polydectes," the girl murmured contritely. "I get so bored! Go ahead, sentence him yourself."

The king shook his head unhappily.

"Naa-a-ah! There's no pleasure in it anymore. Just try to control yourself from now on, huh?"

"I will," she promised, snuggling down again.

As they lifted the vaguely struggling man by his arms, Percy gasped in horror. He understood why he hadn't been able to make out any of the prisoner's words—his tongue had been torn out! There were great drying crusts of blood all over his face and still more coming down his chin to his chest. The man was obviously so weak from loss of blood that he could hardly stand by himself, but so terrified by the agonizing imminence of his doom that he had been desperately trying to make himself understood in some way. His hands waved hopelessly and a dreadful tongueless moan kept rolling out of his mouth as he was dragged, his toes plowing thin furrows in the dust of the floor, off to a small room which was probably the execution ante-chamber.

"See?" Menon said to Percy who was feebly massaging his belly. "He tried to influence the jury before trial. From what I hear, they were the soldiers."

It began to make a kind of highly disagreeable sense, Percy decided. Every citizen on the island—soldiers, civilians, policemen, noblemen, whatever—was a potential member of the jury in any criminal case. The fact that these people took the responsibilities of office rather lightly by the standards of the world he had just left was not as important as their right to crowd into any trial and participate in the verdict. Therefore, if you were arrested on Seriphos for an offense, no matter how flimsy the accusation, you must, above all, not protest your innocence. The man who arrested you would be a talesman; and the punishment for violating this particular law was swift and comprehensive. He began to feel a surprising glow of gratitude for the gag that Dictys had stuffed in his mouth. Why, the man had actually been human even though, instead of pulling Percy's tongue out, he had virtually shoved it down his throat!

But how could you defend yourself when people like these brought you to trial?

"Next case!" the king roared. "And let's cut it short. We're all getting hungry and there's a pretty good execution scheduled for after supper. I don't like to keep my people waiting."

"And that's why we call him Good King Polydectes," a woman murmured as Percy was dragged before the throne and flung down hard.

"Charged," a somewhat familiar voice said above his head, "with impersonating a hero, i.e., Perseus, who, according to the legend—"

"I heard the legend, Dictys," his brother said grumpily. "We went all through it in the previous case. Let's find this man guilty too and start to adjourn. I don't know why there

28

are so many Perseus' these days and so few fake Heracles' or Theseus'. I guess it's like anything else; someone starts a fad and before you know what's happened everybody's doing it."

Dictys' curiosity had been aroused. "What do you mean you went all through it in the previous case?"

"Oh, a couple of my soldiers were on duty up on the hills investigating a report that those small-size monsters, the flying ones, you know which I mean . . . ?"

"Harpies? You mean the ones with heads of girls and the bodies, wings and claws of birds, don't you?"

Polydectes sighed. "Those. It's wonderful to have a brother who knows his monsters so well. I get all mixed up whenever I try to keep them straight in my head. I just have a simple rule: if it has no more and no less than two arms, two legs and one head, then it's human. Otherwise, it's a monster."

"That leaves out the golden-skinned Olympians. They're not human either. I don't know exactly what they are, but a lot of people would classify them with the major monsters."

"And a lot wouldn't," the king pointed out. "So there you are. Where exactly it is that you are, I don't know, but— Anyway, there's been a couple of reports lately that these things, these Harpies, have been smuggling contraband into the island from the air and cutting into the royal revenues of Seriphos. I sent a squad up to Mount Lassus to look into the matter. They were settling down to a little meal before going into action when this man came blundering down the hill. They arrested him as soon as he told them he was Perseus. After they arrested him, of course, and he still tried to argue, they punished him on the spot for jury-tampering under my edict of last summer. Now, I felt they might have been a bit too zealous, but— What is this fellow still doing here? Didn't we find him guilty?"

"Not yet," Dictys assured him. "You haven't asked the jury. But that's all right. I'm in no hurry."

"Well, I am." The monarch spread his hands out at his eager people. "Guilty, eh?"

"Oh, sure!"

"Guilty ten times over!"

"His crimes show in his face, every one of them!"

"Hooray for Just King Polydectes!"

29

Just King Polydectes beamed. "Thank you, my friends, thank you. Now, as for the sentencing—"

Percy leaped to his feet. "What kind of a trial is this anyway?" he raged. "You might give a man a chance for his life!"

King Polydectes shook his head in amazement. He leaned forward to stare at Percy closely, almost squashing a feminine footstool who had just begun to stretch. He was as large as his brother but, since his waist competed burstingly with his height, the effect was overpowering. Also, while most of the people on the island—male and female—seemed to dress in a negligent sheepskin or sagging loincloth, the two royal brothers wore richly dyed woolen garments and the king sported what must once have been a clean tunic of the finest linen.

"I don't know what's upset you, young fellow, but you've had all the chance for your life that the laws of Seriphos allow. Now, why don't you be quiet about it and take your punishment like a man?"

"Listen, please listen!" Percy begged. "Not only am I not a citizen of Seriphos, but I'm not even a citizen of this world. All I want is the chance of finding a way back, practically anything that—"

"That's the whole point," the king explained. "Our laws are not made for citizens—at least not the ones about cooking over a slow fire. Citizens who go wrong get thrown off cliffs or strangled outside the walls at high noon, things like that. Only non-citizens get punished this way. This is how I keep my people happy to be under my rule. Now do you understand? Let's not have any more trouble, huh? Let's be grown-up about paying the penalty for our crimes."

Percy grabbed at his hair, pulled out an exasperated clump and jumped on it. "Look, the way this whole thing started—I won't begin with Mrs. Danner—it's impossible, insane to stand here and watch what— Just a minute." He took a deep breath, conscious of the necessity to remain calm, to be very, very persuasive—to be, above all, *reasonable*. "There was a slight misunderstanding when I met your brother. A sea-serpent—" he paused for a moment, took a deep breath and went on "—an honest-to-gosh real sea-serpent came up to me in my—in my floating chest and welcomed me as the

30

son of Danae. So when I was asked by Dictys who I was—"

"You needn't go on," Polydectes advised him. "The testimony of a sea-serpent is not admissible evidence."

"I was not talking—"

"What I mean is, it's not admissible evidence from the sea-serpent himself. So it certainly is not admissible when you repeat it to us."

"All I was trying to say—"

"Of course," the king stuck out his lower lip and nodded his head thoughtfully, "if it was a land serpent, it might be a little different matter."

Percy paused in the midst of a frantic peroration, intrigued in spite of himself. "It would?" he asked curiously.

"Certainly. Depending on the exact type of land serpent. The oracular type, now, we'd certainly listen to what a pythoness has to say with a good deal of respect. Or the very intelligent and friendly walking kind the legends tell about. But none of this applies to you. You're charged with impersonating Perseus and circulating the impression that you have the courage to kill the Gorgon. For such a crime, a sea-serpent is no good as a character witness. Besides, you've already been found guilty."

"I'm not even arguing with the idea that—"

"Dictys," the king said with a gesture of infinite weariness. "Rule him out of order."

An enormous fist came down on the top of Perseus' head. He felt as if his brains had been rammed down his nostrils. When he could see clearly again through the reddish haze, he was grabbing at the floor which seemed to be curling away from him.

"I don't see why we can't have two executions the same day," Dictys was saying angrily. "Both of these men claimed to be Perseus. As you said, we're having a regular rash of this impersonation lately. Well, a good way to discourage it would be a slam-bang double cooking. A sort of two-course execution. All you have to do is pass sentence on him now, let me attend to details like getting a slave to clean the pot between acts, and—"

"Who's king around here, me or you?" Polydectes roared.

"Oh, you are, you are. But—"

"No buts. You're just a grand duke and don't you forget it, Dictys. Now, I say we'll have just one execution tonight, the man who was caught first. Then tomorrow, we'll have this man in for an official sentencing. It'll give me another excuse to have a throne-room reception, which I like, and will insure that we'll all have something to keep us cheerful on another night."

"All right," Dictys said morosely. "But how many times does it happen that we get two stew-jobs on the same day?"

"All the more reason for spreading them out over a period of time," the king insisted. "Guards, take this man away! You see, Dictys, the way I feel about it is—waste not, want not."

And that, Percy thought bitterly as two huskies with hands like iron claws began dragging him out of the pillared chamber, that's why they call him Philosophical King Polydectes!

At the end of the hall, a grate was abruptly lifted from the floor and he was dropped into the hole like a handful of garbage. The hole was deep enough to knock him out again.

He managed to roll over on his back after a while, nursing his bruises with aching arms. Whatever else was the matter with it—and that came to a good deal!—this was certainly the least gentle of possible worlds.

There was a little light slanting in from the grate. He started to stagger over to it, to get a somewhat better idea of his cell. Something hit him in the stomach and he sat down again.

"You just try that again, mister," a girl's soft voice told him in definite accents. "and I'll really wreck you."

"I beg your pardon?" Percy asked the dead gloom stupidly.

"Don't worry about my pardon. You just stay on your side of the cell and I'll stay on mine. I've had all I want or am going to take of loose-fingered guys who want to find out how much of what a girl has where and don't think twice of finding out right away. I never saw such a place!" Her voice had been riding up the scale with every word; when she came to the last one, she began crying.

After thinking the matter over carefully, Percy started to

32

crawl in the direction of the sobs. "See here . . ." he began gently.

This time she hit him in the eye.

Cursing more fluently than he had ever known he could, he moved to the opposite wall and sat down against it with sternly folded arms. After a while, however, the bitterness got to be too much for silence. He began by cursing the entire human race, limited it to women in general and, after a nod at the girl across from him, he concentrated on Mrs. Danner. He put so much feeling into the business that his maledictions became surprisingly expert, almost worthy of an ecclesiastical body discussing one of their number who had started a campaign to practice the principles of their mutual religion.

He suddenly felt the girl's wet face nuzzling against his shoulder. He leaped into the corner. "Let me tell you, lady," he almost spat out, "that I don't want to touch you any more than—"

"You just mentioned Mrs. Danner's name," she said. "I heard you. Apartment 18-K?"

"Right! But how . . ." Slowly the answer dawned on him. "Oh, you're an alumnus too!"

"I'll kill that woman!" she said through clenched teeth. "The first day I was here, I said I'd beat every dollar bill and every shot of whiskey that she enjoyed on my money out of her if I ever got back. The second day, I said if I only got back I wouldn't pay any attention to her, I'd be so busy kissing things like city sidewalks and big six-foot cops and plumbing equipment. The third day, I didn't think of her at all, I was so busy trying to remember what it was like in the city. But today I know I'm not going back, not ever, so all I do is pray that somehow I will figure out a way of killing her, that somehow—"

She began crying again, great gusty sobs that sounded as if her shoulders were being torn out of place.

Very, very gingerly, the young man returned to her side and patted her on the back. After a while, he took her in his arms and caressed her face gently. Some terribly rough garment she was wearing irritated his own scratched skin.

"It could be worse," he assured her, although privately he wondered what miracle would be necessary to achieve that

33

state. "It could be a lot worse, believe me. Meanwhile, we've found each other. Things won't be nearly so bad with someone to talk to. We're compatriots or comtimeriots or something. My name's Percy S. Yuss. The 'S' stands for Sactrist. I used to own half of a restaurant that our creditors owned two-thirds of. Who are you?"

"Anita Drummond," she said, straightening with a slightly self-conscious giggle and wiping her eyes with her peculiar dress. "Ann. I used to be a ballet dancer. Or, rather, I was still studying to be one, getting a little work here and there. That apartment was a godsend. It just fitted my budget. I plumped myself down in the one chair the place had and gloried in a home at last! Then I notice a piece of parchment on the floor with some poetry on it. I started to read it, stopped, and then began to doze with my eyes on the words. When I woke, I was halfway up a plowed hillside, the chair didn't have any legs, and some old peasant and his wife were saying spells over me to make me vanish before I put a charm on their crops. As soon as they saw me open my eyes, they both jumped on my head, tied me down and carried me into their hut. And they wouldn't listen to a word I had to say! Uh—by the way, if you want to—to be a little more presentable, there's a pile of castoff clothes in that corner there."

Percy ambled over and found a half-dozen badly worn sheepskin tunics. He selected one which smelled strongly but seemed to have fewer inhabitants than the others, and came back. Somehow, wearing clothes again helped restore his confidence. He hadn't had much opportunity to think about the various aspects of nudism since his arrival *sans* wardrobe in this thoroughly mad world, but he felt for the first time that there was a possibility of outwitting his captors now that he was dressed almost as well as they.

Ann continued her story. She was describing how all the inhabitants of a village on the far side of the island had been called into a conference on methods of disposing of the witch.

"There was a real tug-of-war going on between the drive-a-stake-into-her-and-be-done-with-it school and the burn-her-and-then-only-then-can-you-be-sure faction, when a seneschal or chamberlain or whatever he was of King Polydectes court happened to pass by. He was out hunting some small monsters. Furies, I think. Or perhaps they were Sirens. He saw me and before any of the village could say anything, he—Percy, look!"

He jerked his head around to follow her pointing finger. Dusk had been sliding down over the grating at a steeper and steeper incline. There was little more than the most delicate of rosy glows from a sun which had done more than its share of shining and wanted only to rest.

There was a man's head on the other side of the grating. His fingers pressed hard upon his lips. Percy nodded to show that he understood. Slowly the man faded, like smoke dissipating under a gentle summer breeze. Then he was gone.

But the grate lifted slowly, silently, and closed again in a moment. Percy had the eerie sensation of something very heavy that was floating down in the lazy circles that a feather would assume. Without thinking about it, he covered Ann's mouth with his own hand. Even so, her gasp was almost audible when, abruptly, a man wearing a suit vaguely reminiscent of renaissance Italy appeared before them.

He made an adjustment on the extremely thick metal-studded belt he wore, gave them the slightest inclination of his head by way of greeting, and said: "My name is Hermes."

Ann removed Percy's hand from her mouth. "Hermes!" she whispered. "The messenger of the gods!"

"Exactly."

The smile came and went so fast on that aristocratic face that Percy was not quite sure it had ever been. He stared closely at the man's visible skin in the almost non-existent light. It looked golden. "Weren't you the fellow in the white mantle who disappeared when Dictys began asking you questions?"

Hermes nodded. "I suspected who you were, but I had to check on the so-called chest before I could be sure. I could hardly ask you questions while you were surrounded by that mob."

"What questions?" Percy asked eagerly.

"Questions which would determine whether you were the rightful Perseus, the legendary hero who is to save the world from the Gorgon race."

"Look, mister, that stuff has me in enough hot water already! My name is Percy S. Yuss. I am not the son of Danae —we never even had a Daniel in the family anywhere. I don't know this Gorgon everyone keeps raving about all the time and, if I did, I certainly wouldn't feel like killing her. I have nothing against any Gorgon, or any man—except for that fat old slob of king—"

"You're speaking too loudly," the other warned. "It's not any Gorgon we sent you against—it's Medusa herself!" His voice dropped almost to inaudibility at the name. "I spoke to Professor Gray and described the articles with which you had arrived, and he agreed that you must be a man of his own time."

"You mean there's someone else here from the twentieth century?" Ann asked eagerly.

"Where is he? In trouble too?" Percy inquired. He was slightly bitter.

The stranger smiled. This one was long and slow, and Percy decided he didn't like it any better than the fast take. "No, he's not in trouble. He's waiting for you to give you advice on how best to conquer the Gorgon."

"Well, he'll have to run pretty far and awfully fast. I don't like the way everyone jumps when they mention that character. I don't feel like a hero and I don't intend to be one. I've been a sucker all my life, always taking somebody else's falls, but this is one that my mother's favorite son is not going to take."

"Not even to avoid the stew-pot tomorrow?"

Percy swallowed. He'd forgotten the trial according to the laws of Seriphos since he had met Ann. Yes. There'd be another evening like this one, and then he'd be led out—

Could any risk he'd run be greater than the horrible certainty he faced in twenty-four hours? He'd seen enough of these ancient Greeks to have developed a very healthy respect for their deadly efficiency in the prosecution of what they considered to be criminal cases. It was very doubtful, for example, that these people had developed the institution of appeal, or parole. . . .

"Not even," Hermes went on, picking each word up carefully with his teeth and holding it out for them to see, "not even for the chance to return to your own time?"

Ann squealed and the messenger of the gods sternly told

her to be quiet. He jerked at his belt, went invisible. After a while, he turned back on. When he rematerialized, he was staring anxiously up at the grating, one hand poised over his belt.

It struck Percy that this fellow was pretty nervous for a supposed deity. It also struck him that he was being offered just what he needed immediately and most desperately wanted. Did the price he had to pay sound too high? That was silly. Whatever he had to do would be worth the risk and difficulty, if somehow he could find himself back in his own era. Not to mention the desirable aspects of getting out of his present surroundings before supper-time tomorrow.

"I'll do it," he said finally. "Whatever it is you want done, I'll do it. Only listen. Any bargain I made applies to this girl as well as to me."

"Done!" The golden one held out a thin pouch. "Take this. When they lead you to execution tomorrow—"

"Hey! I thought you were going to get us out of this jam. Why can't you just take us with you?"

Hermes shook his head violently. He seemed to be extremely interested in moving on as soon as possible. "Because I can't. You don't have the—the powers. Do what I tell you and you'll be all right."

"Listen to him, Percy!" Ann urged. "This is our only chance. Let's do it his way. Besides, he's a god. He must know his way around this mythological world."

Again Hermes smiled that quick-flitting smile. "When they take you out, make a long speech—as long as you can—about how sorry they are going to be. Whatever it is they're going to have you fight—"

"I'm not going to fight anything," Percy insisted. "I'm going to be—"

"Cooked over a slow fire. I know! But believe me, trust me, you will be led out to fight somebody or something. You make your speech and while you're talking, without anyone seeing you, you dip your hand under your garment and into this pouch. Start fondling the kernels you find there, squeeze them, rub them back and forth between the palm of your hand and the fabric of the pouch. When they start to squirm and move about of their own, get sent in and start fighting as

37

soon as possible! All you do then is to scatter them on the ground all around you—and stand back! Get back as far as—"

He stopped and ripped at the switch on his belt. A torch appeared on the other side of the grating and two heavily whiskered men peered in.

"Could have sworn I saw something," one of them said.

"Well, you can call the guard out and go down to look into it," the other one announced. "Me for the party."

The torchbearer straightened. "Me too. If I saw what I thought I did, I don't want to look into it! Let the morning watch do it."

Out of the darkness came the pouch and pushed itself into Percy's hand. "Remember," they heard the whisper ascending slowly. "Don't start rubbing those kernels too early—and don't wait too long either. Once they begin moving, you've got to get into the fight fast."

The grate lifted briefly, came down again. There was a final whispered injunction: "And don't look into the pouch tonight! Don't even think of touching it until just before you have to!"

They felt a presence departing stealthily above them. Ann moved closer to Percy and he squeezed her reassuringly.

"A big list of don'ts," he grumbled. "Time it just right but don't try to find out what it is! It's like taking a Frenchman up to a row of medicine bottles labeled in Chinese and warning him to take some aspirin before his fever goes up any further, but not to touch the sleeping tablets because they're strong enough to kill him. What does he think I am?"

Ann leaned on him, chuckling with a slight edge of hysteria. "Do you know, Percy, this is the first, absolutely the first ray of hope I've seen since coming to this awful world? And you're grumbling because the directions aren't so clear!"

"Well, after all," his mind said logically—but privately!—"I'm the one who's going to have to fight the Gorgon!"

"I'm not really complaining," he said aloud as they sat down. "But confused directions irritate me. I always feel I'm being taken for a ride."

"Think of sitting in a restaurant," she murmured dreamily. "Or a hairdresser's. Think of going to those chic little dress shops along the Avenue and feeling all those wonderful fabrics and imagining yourself in all those lovely new styles. And all the time making believe that you're really fooling the sales girl into believing you have enough money to buy them. And any time a man you don't like makes a pass at you, you can make him stop. And if he doesn't stop, you yell, and when you yell, you get help instead of him. Oh, civilization, *civilization!*"

She was asleep in his arms. Percy patted her tenderly and prepared to go to sleep himself. He'd had a long, tiring day. Long? Just three thousand years or so!

Unfortunately, he hadn't fallen completely asleep when the execution started. Being underground somewhat and a good distance away, he couldn't see very much. But a good deal of the noise carried. . . .

It was quite a few hours before he finally dozed off and stopped thinking about the man who had come charging down a hillside insisting he was Perseus. How many Perseus' were there in this world? It looked almost as if someone wanted the Gorgon killed very badly indeed and was sending in a good many pinch-hitters.

Who was the real Perseus? He didn't know, but it struck him then that he did know he wasn't. And he was the only one committed so far to killing the Gorgon. What, exactly, was the Gorgon? That was another good question. . . .

Their cell had a third occupant by morning. Agesilaus.

"What did you do?" Percy asked him as he stretched painfully.

"Nothing," the old man said. He sat against the wall hunting for lice in his beard. Every time he caught one, he grinned and cracked it noisily between his teeth. "I'm here because of my brother."

"What do you mean because of your brother?"

"He committed high treason last night and had his brains knocked out according to the law the king made up a few minutes after he committed it. The king was still pretty sore, though, so he passed another law making all blood relatives co-responsible in cases of high treason. I was the only blood relative, so here I am. I'm due to get my brains knocked out today."

"Good old 'waste not, want not' Polydectes," Percy mused.

"What kind of high treason did your brother commit that the king had to pass a law covering it?"

Agesilaus pored through the bottom tattered fringes of his beard. From the obvious disappointment with which he put them aside, it was clear that he considered them devoid of life. "Well, sir, my brother was the royal chef. So of course he was also the public executioner. Somewhere along the line, he must have made a mistake last night. He probably forgot to grease it properly. Because after the execution, the great cooking pot cracked."

"Cracked? You mean they can't use it any more?"

"That's just what I do mean. Broke open like a nut. Ah, you can smile, but let me tell you—that pot was the pride of Seriphos! It wasn't made of bronze or silver or gold, but— and I don't ask you to believe this—of pure *iron!* Yes, sir, this whole island wouldn't be wealthy enough to buy another pot like that. Years and years it took, in my great-grandfather's day, melting down those little meteors that our people had been collecting for generations. And at that they say it was one of the walking reptiles that finally did the casting. Do you blame King Polydectes for getting mad at my brother and all his kith and kin? I don't. Why, his predecessor, King Aurion—the one Polydectes stabbed in the back at the feast of the summer solstice—Aurion would have extended the penalties to relatives by marriage and most of the criminal's close friends."

Percy sat musing on Hermes' prediction of the night before. In all probability, it was not so much an example of accurate prophecy as a clear case of sabotage. He chuckled. Well, at least that particular fear was no longer to be lived with!

"What were these walking reptiles?" Ann asked. She'd been sitting quietly by Percy's side all through his interrogation of the old man, and had pressed his hand when he chuckled to show that she too was hoping that the rest of Hermes' promises would be realized.

"That's a hard question to answer," Agesilaus said slowly. "They must have died off completely forty, fifty years ago. In my great-grandfather's day, there were very few of them left, and they got fewer all the time. They were like the pythonesses who work with the oracles or some of the friendlier sea-serpents. But they were smarter than any of them. And they had legs—some say they even had arms—and they walked about and performed wonders. Taught us how to make pottery, my grandfather told me, and how to—"

"Hey, Agesilaus!"

They all looked up to see the rope ladder come twirling down into the cell. The burly man at the top gestured impatiently to the new arrival. "Time for boom-boom. Hurry up, will you? There's going to be a bull-baiting this afternoon and we have to clear up the arena."

"Their lives are certainly one mad round of pleasure," Ann said bitterly to Percy. "Something doing all the time!"

"Don't misunderstand us," the old man pleaded as he began to mount the ladder. "We have entirely too many people on this island and there haven't been any wars or serious pestilences for over two generations now. What better way to cut down our numbers than by interesting executions? Polydectes calls this 'Population Control with a Smile.'"

"He would," Percy muttered. "That's why we call him Humorous King Polydectes."

Later he was ordered up the rope ladder in his turn and sentenced to combat in the theater with such monsters as would be made available by the zoo superintendent. Polydectes was evidently too morose to develop much interest even in the throne-room reception which a sentencing made inevitable. He lounged sideways on his concubine-infested seat, scowling at the wall, while a court official lackadaisically informed Percy of what he was to expect.

He was sitting thoughtfully in the execution ante-chamber touching the pouch under his sheepskin tunic from time to time, when Ann was hurled in.

"Monster-bait too," she nodded at him. "They're going to send us in together. Let us hope and pray that Hermes knows what he's talking about."

"How come you're under sentence too? What did you do? Not that you can't be tossed into Condemned Row for just making the serious error of being alive."

"Well, you see, I was brought here originally from the

41

other side of the island to become a part of Polydectes' harem."

"How did you get out of that?"

"I didn't get out of it. I'm afraid I just didn't make the grade. The king said I wasn't pneumatic enough. Although," she added with a vicious snap of her teeth. "I still think it was that jealous cat Tontibbi that poisoned his mind against me. Oh no, you don't have to look so startled, Percy," she laughed. "I didn't want to be a member of that harem at all. But it kind of hurts a girl's feelings to be told she's not good enough, when she sees all kinds of fat and sloppy creatures positively infesting the place!" She curled up beside him, still fuming.

In the late afternoon, they were given a handful of dried fruits and, while they were still munching this highly uninteresting supper, were ordered out for execution.

Percy was intrigued to see Ann for the first time in daylight. He noted with approving interest that she was one of those rare and perfect blondes whose skin is so magnificently clear as to neutralize the brightness of her hair into an overall glow of fairness which yet leaves rich hints of darker tones and deeper wells of personality beneath.

They clasped hands as they marched along a constantly curving lane that meandered around the hill on the far side of the citadel. It came eventually to a collection of stone buildings that was obviously the zoo. They were hurried past this, both of them quite happy to be moving fast after a hurried glimpse of what the cages contained. They found themselves in a small valley formed by several tiny hills.

There were seats carved out of the soil of the hills; most of these were already filled. Percy was almost certain he saw Hermes in one of the seats. At the bottom of the valley an area had been surrounded by a high stone wall. There were ponderous gates on either side.

Ann and Percy were alternately pushed and led to one of these gates which was tended by a pair of jumpy youths who held it slightly ajar. Percy nervously reached for the hidden pouch. Everyone was waiting for the king.

He arrived finally, accompanied by his twittering retinue. "Let the punishment proceed," he said in a flat, tired voice. It

42

was evident that he expected little of life now that the execution pot was gone.

Percy dipped his left hand into the pouch as a green-coated bronze sword was shoved into his right. The two boys started to pull the gates back. "I think you'd better start," Ann whispered.

He nodded. "O mighty King Polydectes of Seriphos!" he howled so suddenly that one of the youths dropped his door-ring and turned to run. The Captain of the Guard pushed him back sternly. "I beg and implore you to grant me one last favor." The *kernels* were disagreeably soft to the touch.

Polydectes waved a hand unhappily. "If it's reasonable. And if you can tell me in just a few more or less well-chosen words." He leaned back irritably.

Grinding the soft little bits slowly between his fingers and against the fabric of the pouch, Percy wondered how, where to begin. Suddenly he smiled.

"You are probably wondering whether what happened to your execution pot yesterday was an accident, or whether some discontented subject was responsible for destroying the glory of Seriphos. I alone know the answer, and my request hinges on that."

"He's hooked!" Ann whispered delightedly. "Perfect, Percy, perfect!" A buzz of excitement had ripped up and down the theater's earthen rows.

"Well," the young man went on, massaging and squeezing inside the pouch as if he were a prizefighter trying to build up the powers of his fist, "let us examine what probably happened in terms of the basic function of the pot—cooking. What do we know of the effects of previous ingredients upon the structure of the pot? Do we know anything."

The king looked confused and anxious at the same time, as if he felt that Percy had made a very important point but didn't know precisely what he had made it out of. Even the guards who surrounded them had the half-thrilled, half-frightened appearance of men who believe they stand on the brink of tremendous revelation. Percy was not quite certain whether he had felt a ripple of life on his fingertips; he decided, after a moment of waiting, that he hadn't, and continued rolling *non sequiturs*:

43

"Well, first of all we have sandwiches. On the menu, made to order and to go. We have various kinds of cheese sandwiches. Grilled cheese, cheese and tomato, cheese and bacon, cheese and ham. We can grill them together or separately."

He stopped as he felt a few of the tiny little lumps begin to curl around his fingers.

"If what you're trying to tell me," the king said slowly and intently, "is that my people have been illegally using the state execution pot for grilling cheese and tomato—"

"I'm not trying to tell you anything," Percy said curtly. "Let's get on with the execution."

"No, listen son," Polydectes said warmly, "you were making sense. It was a little hard to follow, but you had a good solid point there. Somewhere, anyway. Please go on."

"Yes, do go on," one of the spectators called out. "I can understand you."

"There's nothing to understand!" He was feeling desperate. The *kernels* were leaping about in the pouch like tiny frogs frightened out of their pond. "I have nothing to tell you. I made everything up. I just wanted a delay. Now will you go on with the execution?"

"We will not!" the king said portentously. "You're trying to protect somebody. Somebody important."

The little writhing bits were now grouped at the mouth of the pouch, burrowing out to freedom. Percy looked at Ann's anxious face, saw that she understood his predicament but had no way to help him.

"Listen, Polydectes," he said hoarsely. "Why don't you give the throne to someone who's deserved it from away back? Tontibbi would make a better ruler several times over. Not only is she smarter than you, not only does she know more about civilized living, but she also—"

"Open those gates," roared Purple King Polydectes, "and throw him to the beast!"

The great portals creaked back. Ann and Percy were pushed out into the enormous sweep of stone floor. Ann managed to keep her balance, but Percy, thrown off by the arm he had been keeping under his tunic where the pouch lay against his breast, staggered forward unable to lift his head and regain his equilibrium. He tripped and came crashing

44

down on one hand and one knee, his sword ringing on the flagstone as it spun out of his grip.

He heard Ann scream in disbelief and looked up. Racing toward them from the other gate was something that belonged on an insane artist's drawing board and nowhere else.

Waist-high it was, but over twelve feet wide, a weirdly fused conglomeration of canine, lupine, reptile, human and something else, something, Percy immediately felt, that this planet had never bred. The thing ran on the bodies of snakes, lizards, dogs and wolves, all of them seemingly independent living entities and all of them nonetheless joined to the main body by thick trunk-like appendages which took the place of their hind ends. Six distinct heads the thing had, each of them, including the human one, with dripping jaw thrown wide open and screaming an unrecognizable counterpoint to each other.

It was moving terribly fast. Percy leaped to his feet and, withdrawing the handful of writhing lumps from the pouch, darted toward the terrified girl.

He pulled her behind him before making his throw. A gaping crocodile mouth which had been wavering toward them was abruptly withdrawn as one of the bits fell upon it. Percy managed to throw them in a rough semi-circle, then, pushing Ann ahead, stumbling, bouncing against her and running in crazy zig-zags because of the looks he kept throwing over his shoulder, he made it to the opposite wall.

They stood awed at the destruction they had let loose.

The little lumps had been kernels all right. But of such plants as only the most unholy gardener could have sown!

Wherever the seeds touched a surface, they grew—grew luxuriantly! And in a matter of seconds had put forth on their sickly white stems elephant-sized white flowers covered with irregular purple blobs. Their roots tore into and through the surface contacted like streams of flood water irresistibly seeking their way. Tremendously hungry the roots had to be to support such fantastic growth in the rest of the plant and tremendously hungry they were. Whatever they touched died on the spot—flesh grew bloodless, normal plants turned yellow with sudden age and lack of chlorophyll, the very stone

45

flaked and crumbled into fine dust under the probing requisitions of the sprouting root hairs.

They grew, these seeds, with the maintained momentum and direction in which Percy had thrown them. They reproduced by means of single new seeds virtually expectorated ahead by each fruitful flower.

The monster, which had turned to run, was engulfed in mid-stride and dropped in a moment—a pallid husk. The walls of the stadium, too—those on the side at which Percy had thrown the seeds—were powdered ruins in a moment. And the entire audience, after a horrified moment of half-understanding, had risen and fled before this botanical juggernaut.

They could have stayed. It hardly reached the top rows.

Almost, it seemed, a moment after it had started to live, it became morimund. It was as if tremendously hungry of life, it could find in this place or this world no life on which to feed, nothing whose constitution was what it needed to sustain itself. By the time that the forward blossoms were pluming open among the rapidly emptied seats, their ancestors of seconds ago on the stadium floor had turned a brittle black and begun to fall apart.

In a few minutes, except for the transparent outline of the monster lying near the dissolved gate which it had been vainly trying to regain, and the completely disintegrated length of wall over which the blossoms had passed, there was no sign of the weapon which Hermes had given Percy. A thin grey fog wandered away blindly—and that was all.

There was the abrupt sound of heels striking the ground. They turned. Hermes appeared, a slightly mocking smile on his expertly carved face.

"Well?" he asked. "Was that satisfactorily efficient, Perseus?"

"My name is Percy," the young man told him shortly. "And with that kind of power I don't see why you don't go after the Gorgon yourself."

"Your name, for the duration of this bargain, my friend, is Perseus as far as the Olympians are concerned. With regard to power," he shrugged, "there are many different kinds. Some so old that they can be conquered only at the cost of universal destruction. Some so new," he smiled brilliantly at the two of them, "that their scope cannot as yet even be estimated. And there is the power of a legend which says a truth that must be fulfilled before the days of a world can further unwind." He nodded, in what seemed to be a prodigious self-satisfaction. "Now, if you two would kindly clasp my waist from either side, we can go on."

The thought occurred to Percy that he was remarkably cool and chipper away from the dungeons of King Polydectes. The touch of aristocratic insolence in his manner was much deeper now than it had been the previous night when he had broken it frequently to gnaw a nervous lip at the grating above. With weapons such as he had at his disposal, why should he worry about the soldiers of a monarch as petty as Polydectes?

Could it be because the weapons were very limited in quantity and could be used only for emergencies—or to make such important bargains with people like himself as the Olympians deemed necessary? And why was it necessary to make bargains with a master hash-slinger like Percy S. Yuss? For all of Hermes' chatter about different kinds of power, it still seemed much more logical for the Olympians to knock off Medusa themselves than to provide an ordinary human with the weapons to do it.

If they could provide the weapons to do it. If they could . . .

He shook his head in bewilderment and grabbed Hermes' waist as Ann had already done, his arms overlapping hers. The golden one flexed his shoulders for a moment, then touched the belt lightly.

They rose, not abruptly, but with the steady insistence of a warm updraft. At two or three hundred feet, Hermes made another adjustment and began skimming south at a fair rate of speed. It wasn't difficult to maintain a grip and, since the late day was extremely mellow, this particular kind of flight was very enjoyable. Percy and Ann smiled, "Fun, isn't it?" at each other.

"This is some kind of anti-gravity belt, isn't it?" Percy asked.

Hermes gave him a brief, cold glance. "Don't ask such questions!" he said with the insulting emphasis of an order. He flexed his shoulders again and stared straight ahead.

47

Percy bit his lip. He definitely didn't like this character. . . .

They came down on a little peninsula on the southern tip of Seriphos. There, beside a long rock-like shelf that overhung the sea, was a small and neat hut built of driftwood. After separating themselves from Hermes, the two stood uncertainly on the path for a moment.

"Professor Gray," called out the golden man. "Your fellow-tourists!"

A highly energetic little old man dressed in a grey flannel suit came prancing out of the hut. "Hello, hello!" he said chirpingly. "Come inside, please do. I've been waiting quite a while for you, young fellow. Thank you very much Hermes, you'll be back tomorrow?"

"If we can get the boots working right." The messenger shot up and away at several times the speed he had used in bringing them there.

Professor Gray took a hand of each and hauled them into his hut. "Now, sit down and make yourselves comfortable. Dinner will be ready in a moment." He indicated a full-bellied pot bubbling in the fireplace. Percy, remembering another such pot and noticing the resemblance in all but size, smiled wryly.

"What is it?" the other man asked. Despite his age, he had the quick gestures of a highly nervous sparrow. "What are you brooding about? You must tell me all your adventures, both of you."

So they did. All through dinner.

"I'm sorry. Truly sorry." Professor Gray had his hands shoved deeply into his pockets. "I had no idea—no idea at all —that my little experiment would be dragging fellow humans into such misery. My deepest apologies to both of you, especially the young lady," he asserted self-consciously. "And I certainly didn't intend to present Mrs. Danner with the equivalent of a lifetime pension."

"What little experiment?" Percy asked curiously.

"You mean to tell us that you were the first one through?" Ann asked, her eyes very wide.

"I'm afraid I mean just that." The little man walked bouncingly up and down the length of the small hut. "You

48

see, when I retired as Head of the Classics Department at the University, I rented that apartment as a sort of laboratory. I felt it was the place where I might try some experiments with my theories of subjective time-travel, theories based more upon the ancient Greek philosophers than on our modern mathematicians. There, I thought I'd be alone, safe at least from ridicule. The only thing I didn't anticipate quite so early was my success! Simply because it is a period about which little is known by our archaeologists, I fixed my psyche during the experiment upon the time of the *older heroes,* so called. For the purpose, I used a poem by Pindar, written nine centuries after the period in which I was interested. I copied an English translation of the poem on a piece of sheepskin, to create greater subjective verisimilitude. I didn't have any warning, either, the day I sat down to try just another experiment in mental control of time."

He grinned at them, gestured with both palms. "Much to my surprise, I—well, I fell in! I was more fortunate than either of you in that I had a plentiful supply of silver and copper coins when I arrived in the southern, less densely populated half of the island. It was inevitable that I should arrive in Seriphos, by the way, because of the poem celebrating Perseus' return here after he had acquired the Gorgon's head that I had used as a psychic time-travel tie. I was able to develop a reputation as a kind of beneficent local wizard through my knowledge of the people and the time. And I've done fairly well for a scholar most of whose adult life has been spent in other places than the press and scramble of business: I own this hut and a substantial tract of productive land. By the standards of this community, I am quite a wealthy man.

"But there is my greatest compensation here—the close, on-the-spot study of a period which has always fascinated me. I place it, by the way, somewhere between the end of the Mycenaean and the beginning of the Achaean eras of Greek history. Roughly 1400 B.C. It was a remarkable time in that, while superstition flourished, religion—important both before and after this period—was almost nonexistent. Some scholars even claim—"

"Pardon me, sir," Percy broke in, "but how did we come to follow you?"

"I think the answer is obvious. The parchment, containing the English translation of the poem which served me as a kind of target, was still in the apartment. So, therefore, was my subjective aura. And there had also been created what might be called a psycho-chronological hole in the place through which I had fallen. You young people were unfortunate enough to read the poem under these conditions and therefore followed me, arriving more or less in my neighborhood, depending on personality differences in relation to the psycho-chronological hole. I think the apartment should be fairly safe now, since Percy had the parchment in his hand when he arrived and dropped it in the Aegean Sea."

"And here we are," Percy mused. "In the world of Greek mythology."

Professor Gray shook his head emphatically. "I beg your pardon, but we most definitely are not. There never was such a place! It's entirely a world in Man's imagination. You are in a time that is to give rise to what we call Greek mythology. The actual events in this era will be the religion and mythos of the next. What form exactly they will take I cannot say, since this is not our world nor our universe."

"What do you mean?" Percy's question was fringed with sudden panic.

"I mean that you aren't in the past at all. You are in the future, uncountable eons in the future! This is the formative period of Greek mythology on another Earth, in a space-time universe which came into being only after our own grew senile and died. Much the same things are happening to it and on it as happened to our own planet but, since it is not the same Earth, the results tend to be more and more different."

"The—the future?" Ann shook her head as if to clear it of accumulating webs. "Another space-time universe?"

"Is it really so hard to understand or believe? It isn't possible to travel backwards in time, only ahead of one's era. The past, having died, is dead forever: only the future is constantly unrolling. Since I hurled myself into this particular period which, being in the past, had ceased to exist, I inevitably materialized in a parallel period in the succeeding cos-

50

mos. The ancient philosopher Anaximander of Miletus was one of the first to discuss the concept of an *Indefinite-Infinite* from which all things were drawn, including primordial atoms and planetary systems, super-galaxies and even time-streams. There is birth and death in all things, said Anaximander, and they perish into those from which they have been born. Thus there were Earths in space-time universes which existed long before our own and, barring unexpected developments in Anaximander's Indefinite-Infinite, there will be Earths in many, many succeeding space-time universes."

"And in each one," Percy muttered slowly as he began to understand. "In each one, another Perseus."

"Right!" Professor Gray beamed. "Except that he does not necessarily do the same things in the same way each time. But enough of this metaphysics! You young people are exhausted: suppose I show you to your beds. You begin a training program tomorrow, Percy—you, especially, will need your sleep."

He led Ann up a ladder into a narrow bedroom in the loft which, after her recent accommodations, she found magnificent. Percy and he bedded down near the fireplace on a soft pile of skins.

"Look, professor," Percy asked as the older man extinguished the torch, "if this isn't a world of actual mythology, then those babies aren't really gods and monsters. Yet, I saw a monster in the arena which I'd like to forget for the sake of my dreams, and I can remember other things which are even harder to explain."

"Of course. And if that thing—it was a scylla, by the way —had caught you— But while they are real, painfully so, they don't come from our universe at all."

"How's that?"

"There are universes which adjoin ours in the plenum. Every possible type of universe exists parallel with ours. Many of them have Earth-type planets and Sol-type suns positioned in their space to correspond with ours. Well, it happens that the sub-spatial fabric separating these universes from each other is understandably weak in their youth and grows progressively stronger as the ages pass. At one time, there was probably a constant exchange and pilgrimage of individuals taking place from one universe's 'Earth' to another.

51

Right now, it is down in all probability to the barest of trickles as the sub-spatial fabric has solidified and lets little through in any place. In a little while, it will have closed or clotted completely and all that will be left will be the memories of strange unearthly creatures to generate beautiful legends and peculiar superstitions."

Percy grunted as he chewed into the strange texture of this information. "Then the gods aren't gods at all, I guess, but what I heard one of the men who captured me call them: Olympian monsters."

"Well, yes. Monsters, in the sense that they are nonhuman intrinsically since they evolved on a different world. But, Percy, they are very like us in so many ways! They are much more advanced scientifically at this point than is our race, and they can't be as confusingly horrible in their thought processes—no matter how bad they might get!—as—well, the Gorgon race for example. These creatures are humanoid: they therefore must come from a world and universe whose natural laws are very much like our own: and they are very much interested in helping humanity advance to their level. The people of this time call them Olympian monsters, by the way, because in our world they originate upon Mount Olympus in Northern Thessaly.

"I owe the one called Hermes a good deal: if it hadn't been for his help, I wouldn't have nearly a third of the wealth and knowledge I do. He sought me out shortly after I arrived and insisted on doing all sorts of useful little favors. I'll admit to feeling the same sort of distrust for a while which, I can see, you are experiencing. But believe me, it will be washed away by the fellow's ubiquitous friendliness! I just can't understand why later myths gave him the character of a mischievous schemer! Of course, it's entirely possible that the myths which will evolve in this world will be greatly different from the ones in our own." He nodded to himself gravely, with his head cocked at an angle, as if he were enviously imagining the kind of Greek myth with which some future Professor of Classics should have to deal.

"The Gorgon race is pretty bad in comparison, huh? If I'm going to chase over to—to—"

"Crete. Their headquarters is on the island of Crete."

"Well, can you give me some idea of what they're like?"

Professor Gray sat up, supporting his chin on his knees with his cupped hands. "I can, but please remember that what I know is a combination of archaeo-anthropological data and what I have learned about present conditions from Hermes. Almost all the more disgusting monsters, he has explained, are properly speaking members of the Gorgon race who are themselves, however, basically reptile. The Gorgons derive from a universe or universes so different from our own even in the laws of biology and chemistry as to be virtually beyond our comprehension. Their chieftainess, for example, has a human body and a head covered with writing snakes. Which jibes, of course, with the description of Medusa in almost all the texts.

"The only thing," he said, his delicate old face wrinkling suddenly, "that bothers me a little is the exact relationship of Medusa to the cult of the Snake-Goddess or All-Mother of ancient, matriarchal Crete. In fact, by middle Mycenaean times—just before the present era—the religion of the Triple Goddess, as she was then called, was being practiced over almost the entire Mediterranean by priestesses who not only dominated the community but had control of all agriculture and most of local industry. In the records of our world, this religion disappeared suddenly, to be replaced by the Olympic pantheon. Yet, here, in a parallel transitional period, some two centuries before the Homeric heroes, there is no sign of either religion. Very strange. Possibly neither has developed as yet; although I would give a good deal to see what conditions are like on Crete. Hermes tells me that since the Gorgons have been crowding in, the island is far too dangerous to visit on a purely social basis. Yet— Yet—

"And then there's the question of the Gorgons' reptilian form. Among the majority of ancient peoples, the serpent was the symbol of wisdom and fertility. Not until the Genesis of our Bible do we find a less flattering picture of the snake and, even then, he is still incredibly shrewd and cunning, though no longer friendly to Man. Is it possible, now—"

Percy, exhausted by his first two days in pre-Achaean Greece, fell asleep at this point, to dream that he was back in

53

his own time and a clever, fast-talking salesman named Lucifer Beelzebub Hermes had talked him into buying a very expensive restaurant which, upon his assuming ownership, turned out to have a clientele composed exclusively of rattlesnakes who insisted on charging their meals. When he approached one of them with a suggestion that a part of the long-standing bill be paid, the creature lunged at him with an enormous and rapidly-growing set of triple poison fangs.

He was rather bitter when he woke up, even though Ann had prepared a tasty breakfast out of some local bread and cheese and five eggs from as many different types of birds. Also, Professor Gray had laid out some fairly good garments for them.

The fact remained that whatever Medusa was, however dangerous the Gorgons were, he, Percy Sactrist Yuss, was committed to ridding the world of them and would probably, in the process, rid the world of himself.

"Some people," he told Ann morosely, "have lots of different talents. I have only one—being a sucker. But I'm the best sucker, the most complete sucker, that this world—or the one before it—has ever seen. I'm actually a genius at it."

"The trouble with you," she said, surveying him judiciously over an extremely well-designed water jug, "is that you think about yourself too much."

"Well, it's a good idea while there's still enough of me left around to make it worthwhile."

Professor Gray trotted in and insisted on Percy's coming out to test the weapons which Hermes had been bringing for the encounter with the Gorgon. Reluctantly, Percy followed him outside into the still, strong brightness of a morning in the Eastern Mediterranean.

"This is the cap of darkness or invisibility," the little man said, handing him a collection of curved metal plates welded in a rough hemisphere and decorated with many wires and incredibly tiny transformers. "The switch is just under the brim—here!—but you'll have to be very careful about practicing with it since Hermes tells me its power supply is very low and there is little possibility of refueling for a long while. Don't gape like that, Percy, it really does work! I told you that their science was far ahead of ours."

He reached into the large wicker basket for a black object

shaped like an overnight zipper bag. It had a long looping handle. Where the zipper should have been, however, there was instead a thin and hazy line that shut the bag so completely as to make it seem like one continuous piece.

Professor Gray tapped it importantly. "The *kibisis*. The satchel in which you are to place the Gorgon's head after you've cut it off. This is probably the most important single item—except for the boots—that you will be given. You see, according to legend, even after her head has been severed, Medusa still has the power to turn men into stone with a glance. Furthermore, according to Hermes, she is so unlike life as we know it that, merely with her head, she will still be capable of blasting open an ordinary container. This bag can only be opened from the *outside*. You are to place her head in the *kibisis* and keep it there until you hand it over to Hermes. And now for the major item: how are you to get her head in the first place? Well, we have a sword for you, the famous *harpe*."

He was, Percy noted with disgust, speaking with all the patronizing familiarity of a sports enthusiast or a fight manager explaining the virtues of a new defensive crouch to a young championship contender.

"This is big stuff to you, isn't it, professor? Being able to crowd yourself into a story you used to lecture about?"

"Crowd myself? But I am already in the legend! Professor Gray is as much a part of the original story as Percy S. Yuss is Perseus and Ann Drummond is Andromeda. Hesiod refers to the Graiae Sisters who have been gray since birth and who are largely responsible for the equipping of Perseus on his mission to Medusa. Well, there's only one of me and none of it is female, but it's still close enough to the real myth. As, for example, your rescue of yourself and Ann from the scylla, which is classically a monster of whirlpool and shipwreck, tallies with the original tale which has Perseus saving Andromeda from a sea-beast, though only after he's killed the Gorgon. The fact that you did arrive at Seriphos in a bathtub and as an adult contradicts Pherecydes' version in which the infant Perseus, shut inside a chest with his mother Danae, is rescued from the sea by the fisherman Dictys, brother of King Polydectes. And yet it was Dictys' net that pulled you out of the Mediterranean. . . .

"You see it goes on and on agreeing with the legend here, altering it slightly there. That's the fascinating thing about myth," the old academician went on: "there's fact in it somewhere, the trick is to find that little nugget of solidity and be able to recognize it when you do. The truth might be that there was originally a Professor Gray in the actual story as it took place on our world—and his name, sex and . . . quantity were altered by later writers; or, possibly the truth is that there is a repeating myth in every space-time universe, a myth which has several broad generalizations which must be satisfied, but whose particulars may be filled in from almost any palette."

"You mean," Percy asked slowly, reluctantly unclasping a precious hope he had let nobody know about, "that this time Perseus might be killed by the Gorgon instead of vice versa?"

Professor Gray nodded with brain-curdling enthusiasm. "Now you're beginning to understand! Exactly. Don't you see it was always possible, just as it's possible that you aren't the right Perseus any more than I'm the right Gray—or Graiae? That's what makes this whole thing so infernally exciting!"

His pupil started to smile. Unfortunately, since he had great difficulty in lifting the corners of his mouth from under his chin, the attempt was no great success as smiles go. "Yeah," he said. "I'm beginning to see that."

"Here. Try your sword," the professor suggested, his eyes almost popping under the weight of the enormous mass of metal he was holding out to Percy with both straining arms.

Percy took it and, by tearing his back muscles slightly, was able to lay it on the ground before it fell out of his hand.

"Don't tell me I'm supposed to go fence a duel with that girder!"

"Oh, you'll get used to it, you'll get used to it! Notice that it's made of iron, not bronze? Nothing's too good for Perseus!"

"Thanks, pal, from the bottom of my—"

"Of course, in the later vases," the professor had backed-into archaeology again, "especially the red-figure ones, the *harpe* of Perseus is represented in the shape of a sickle. But the earliest kind, the black-figure vases, show it as a straight sword. And a straight sword it must have been because that's how Hermes brought it here to be held against the time when a Perseus arrived."

"Speaking of arrivals," Ann commented from the doorway of the hut, "the 8:45 is coming in on Runway One. Better move back!"

They looked up to see Hermes twirl down from the bright blue sky a little more rapidly than usual. He carried a peculiar and bulky package slung from his belt. He began walking toward them the moment his toe-tips punched the soil.

"Is he ready? I hope he's been practicing with those weapons."

"As a matter of fact," the little old man said, rubbing his forehead, "he just began to examine them. You're a little premature, Hermes: remember, these people only arrived last evening."

The golden-skinned young man nodded absent-mindedly for a moment, then bent to open his package. "I know. Unfortunately, a good deal has changed in the world since then. The Gorgons will be making their final attempt at conquest in the next twenty-four hours. Medusa must be killed before tonight."

"I won't!" Percy raved. "You just can't pull a man out of a nice, comfortable world and expect him to— to—"

"As I recall," Hermes drawled, turning around with a pair of calf-length metallic boots, "I pulled you out of a series of highly unpleasant situations. You were not too comfortable in that underground cell, and you would have been even less so the next day in a certain large cooking vessel which I destroyed. Then, there was the meeting in the arena. . . ."

"Percy's point," said Professor Gray uncomfortably, "is that he has hardly begun to adjust to the situation, psychologically. And physically—well, he's not even able to flourish the sword as yet."

"I'll take care of those difficulties!" the messenger promised. "Here are your boots. When you rub them together like so, your mobility is multiplied by a factor of twenty. Put them on and take a drink of this."

Dubiously, Percy donned the boots that were to make him

twenty times as fast. The soles vibrated underfoot in a way that was not exactly pleasant.

With even more uncertainty, he swallowed some liquid out of a long tubular flask which the golden one held out to him He almost doubled over as the drink hit his stomach like a bursting rocket. "Whee-ew! That's potent stuff!"

A thin, smirking grin. "Wait! You've yet to find out how potent it really is. Now, I want you to pick up your sword, Percy, And remember as you do how strong you've become. Why, you're such a powerful man that I wouldn't be at all surprised to see you wave it around your head like a tiny twig fallen from a dead tree."

Percy reached for the sword, a rather silly grin on his face. It was all very well for Hermes to try to inspire him with such confidence, but he knew his capacity. A sword as heavy as that . . .

Only it was very light. It was the easiest thing in the world to lift and flourish. He did so, marveling at the feel of power in his arm and wrist muscles.

"Wonderful!" Professor Gray breathed. "That flask—does it contain the fabled *Nektar,* the ineffable drink of the gods?"

"After a fashion," the messenger said. "After a fashion. Now that we're all set, Perseus, suppose you gather up your armory and we can start out."

Events got very dim after that. Percy found it hard to remember their sequence. Sometime or other, Ann had come up and said a good deal of angry nonsense to Professor Gray who had seemed very confused. Then, just as she was about to throw her arms about his neck, Hermes took him by the hand and they went soaring away. His head felt a lot clearer when they were high against the clouds, racing southward across an island-dotted sea.

"Why," he said, "don't you people, with all the tremendous stuff you have at your disposal, go after the Gorgon yourself?"

"A matter of prophecy. The legend of Perseus must be fulfilled at all costs." Hermes let the words dribble out of his mouth as he peered ahead anxiously.

Vaguely dissatisfied, Percy found himself wondering if the answer made any sense after all. Like so many of the things

58

he'd been told recently, it sounded as if a small lump of truth had been used to flavor a great steaming bowl of nonsense.

The drink must be making him feel this way, he decided. Professor Gray was an entirely sincere if slightly bumbling human being. Still . . .

"And why did you tell us that we'd get sent back to our own time? According to what Professor Gray says, that time is dead forever."

The golden man shook his head impatiently and they both almost turned over. "Now, now, this is no time to look for problems and disagreements. You need another drink. Here."

He almost forced the flask to Percy's lips. Again there was an explosion in his intestines which, while not so violent as the first, had much more of an echo. He looked at Hermes with new trust and fondness. How could he ever have doubted so splendid a friend?

"Let me tell you what you will see when you force your way into Medusa's chamber," Hermes was saying with a drowse-provoking smoothness. "Medusa herself will appear to be a horrible, horrible . . ."

Under them, the waves raced gleefully through each other, pausing every once in a while to shake a fistful of foam at the constantly watching and disapproving sky. Percy swung lazily from the hands of the steadily talking golden man. Life was simple, he thought, when people told you what to do and what to expect. Everything had become so easy.

He looked up as he felt Hermes let go one of his hands and fumble for the switch on his cap of darkness. A moment later, the same hand made a similar gesture on its owner's wide belt.

"Making us invisible, that's what you're doing," Percy commented, nodding his head slowly.

"Are we there already?"

"Yes. Sh-h-h! Please be quiet!"

Turning his head, he saw a long, greenly rich island expanding up towards them. "Why did you people have to go to so much trouble making this cap for me and all that sort of thing when you could have given me something you already had—like the belt, for example—and I'd have been able to travel here all by myself? What I mean," he went on

59

with large, drunken generosity, "is that you're probably a busy man, Hermes. 'Sa shame for me to drag you away from —"

"Will you shut up?" Hermes' voice was a whispered custard of fear. His eyes flickered up and down, right and left, as they dropped into an enormous, silent city built from massive blocks of grey, moss-covered stone. "We didn't give you a belt for the same reason we gave you a sword instead of a ray-gun. Short supply."

"Sup—supply?" Percy asked stupidly. He scratched his head and almost knocked the cap off.

"Supply. And besides, do you think we're foolish enough to trust a human with our weapons?" Their feet touched the worn surface of a rock balcony high up on a building. Hermes pulled him behind the great finger of stone that served as one of the lintels for the doorway. Percy could feel the twitching tenseness in the body of the golden man as he hugged him to the wall and waited to make certain that no one was coming out on the balcony to investigate.

He tried to remember the last thing that Hermes had said. He found he couldn't and wished desperately that the black blobs in his mind would go away and let him think again. But he remembered that Hermes had made some sort of slip in his fright, that abruptly he had almost had the vision of— of— What?

"You need one more drink before you go inside," came the insistent whisper. Percy started to protest that he had been drinking entirely too much of this strange concoction but, as he did so, Hermes thrust the flask into his mouth. He gagged and managed to dribble the bulk of the liquid down his chest, but enough entered his stomach to provide a walloping accompaniment to the clouds which slid over his thoughts once more.

"Now you know what you are to do. Her bedroom is the first one to the right of the corridor leading away from the balcony. Don't even try to think, Perseus: it will only lead to disaster! All of your instructions are safely buried in your mind; if you just relax and let them take over, you will do exactly the right thing every time. Remember, you can't fail! You cannot fail! Now go!"

Hermes pushed him around the lintel and down the hall.

60

Percy stumbled the first few feet, then managed to walk upright and as steathily as he knew he should. He wanted to turn back and argue some very important points with his guide, but somehow it was much more important to keep walking, to keep one hand on the hilt of his great sword, to have every nerve anxious and waiting. . . .

The hall was covered with tapestry of a fabric so strange that it almost seemed logical for his eyes to be unable to focus whenever he tried to make out the design. The tapestry ended just before an archway supported by spiral stone columns. He walked in.

Almost before he saw the reclining, sleeping figure with the headful of drowsy, slightly restless serpents, he had flipped open the *kibisis* and ground his boots together to close the sub-surface relays. He was speeding toward Medusa at a fantastic rate of speed across an enormous stretch of floor thoroughly as slimy as Hermes had said it would be. And along the walls, his eyes noted—yes, there were chained the groaning, writhing human captives on which the Gorgon race was constantly experimenting. All, all as Hermes had said it would be, droning the picture into his ear as they flew toward ancient Crete above the gaily splashing sea.

He hardly remembered grasping the snakes with one hand and, pulling slightly to extend the neck, lifting the heavy *harpe* behind him. The sword poured down and the chillingly ugly head came free, greasy stinking blood pouring from it. He dropped it into the *kibisis* with the snapping, sideways motion that Hermes had told him to use, flipped the lid shut and turned to run back, exactly as Hermes had told him he should.

But, in that moment before he closed the *kibisis*, a single, frantic thought had sped out of the severed head. It hit his swirling thoughts like a pebble from a sling-shot and sent them rippling in so many directions that he almost came to a full stop.

Almost. But he ran on, shaken by the awful familiarity of that mental voice. It was as if his mother had tearfully asked him to stop, to stop now, this moment, no matter what the consequences. It was as if the wisest men in the world had assembled in convention and passed a resolution addressed to

61

him, formally requesting Percy Sactrist Yuss in the name of humanity and universal intelligence to turn somehow, before he plunged the whole world into disaster. It was as if a million tiny infants had bawled out in a terrible, unendurable agony that he alone had caused.

The voice was safely shut in the *kibisis*, but its dwindling harmonics rang on and on in his mind.

Hermes came around the lintel as he emerged on the balcony and waited for him to rub his boots back into normal speed. Then he held out a hand. "All right, give it to me."

He started to hand the *kibisis* over, but the memory of the thoughts locked inside made him pause for a moment. He swung the black bag from its long, looping handle undecidedly.

The golden-skinned man laughed. "You're not going to keep it?"

Percy didn't know what he was going to do. He certainly didn't want that head of surpassing horror for any reason that he could think of. And, certainly, wasn't he supposed to give the *kibisis* to Hermes as soon as he had filled it with the grisly contents for which it had been designed? Certainly he was. Someone had explained all that to him. But that thought he had received from the head . . .

"Let's not have any trouble, Percy. Give me the bag and we can start back. Your girl friend is waiting."

That was decisive. He still couldn't think as clearly as he would have wished, but he could remember. He recognized Hermes' manner now; the bitterness was still too fresh in him for forgetfulness.

It was the manner of the broker who had sold him the half-interest in a more than half-bankrupt restaurant. Just at the point when he'd started to ask the questions that had been bothering him about a series of bookkeeping entries, the man had shoved a fountain pen in his hand and begun to prattle of the possibility of selling the place the very next week at a tidy profit. "Of course I don't know if you'd be interested in getting rid of it so soon after purchase. I imagine if the profit were sufficiently high, however, you would hardly feel like holding on. Well, Mr. Yuss, as soon as we leave my office, I'll have you meet Mr. Woodward. Mr. Woodward has been interested in purchasing this restaurant for some time and, quite confidentially, I think we can get close to . . ." He had signed almost before he knew he had, and acquired therefrom a piece of property that was more like a cash incinerator than an eating-place.

And he had sworn not to be taken that way again. He recognized Hermes' manner now: it was the con man getting a little impatient at the sucker's delay and throwing out some more bait.

"No," he said. "I won't give it to you until we return. I think I want Professor Gray to look at it first."

He never knew how he realized that the tiny red tube Hermes suddenly flashed was a weapon. He leaped clumsily sideways and the stone wall section in front of which he had been standing exploded like a burst paper bag. He kicked the boot switch into operation and tore the *harpe* out of its back scabbard.

Hermes was turning the ray-gun around at him with the same unpitying, contemptuous smile he had flashed so many times before, when Percy became a darting, feverish flicker of humanity. As the golden man rolled backwards to find a good shot somewhere in this incredibly fast creature who seemed to be one continuous line, his eyes grew wider and wider, his lips pulled in deeper and deeper; a fear ricochetted through him. And, when the screaming sword finally bit his head off, it rolled to the balcony floor looking just like that—thoroughly popped eyes and almost nonexistent mouth shaming the refined gold of the skin and carefully-cut, artistically-designed features.

Percy leaned on his sword and breathed hard. This was the second in one day! He was becoming a wholesaler!

He turned the boots off. He didn't know when he might need that extra speed again in a hurry, and how much fuel they still had left in them. He stepped carefully away from the bleeding, decapitated corpse.

Abruptly the sword grew very heavy; he holstered it with difficulty. The drug was wearing off. He knew it was a drug now as the hypnosis induced by Hermes began to dissipate. The city was still the same quiet stone. But it was no longer the thing of implicit horror it had been up to a few minutes ago. Men lived here, he knew, and went about their tasks in their various human ways.

The building on whose balcony he stood was much older than the others around it. It had a distinctive style of architecture—more pillared stone and friezed decoration than even a palace should have.

He tip-toed back along the hall. There was the tapestry he remembered, except that now he could see it quite clearly. Men and women were dancing around a huge upright snake in one section; in another a great lizard plowed a field while people walked behind it joyfully strewing flowers across the new-made furrows. In the last, a tall and beautiful woman stood before a crowd of young children and allowed a pair of small snakes to curl around her bare breasts.

He paused at the entrance to the room, reluctant to enter and confirm his suspicions. In his hands, the black *kibisis* undulated slowly as if the thing inside it were still alive. Well, there at least Hermes had told the truth.

At last he looked into the chamber. It was a large, clean room lit by three huge torches, very sparsely furnished. There were no chained humans along the walls; there were colorful murals instead which dealt with a strange nonhuman race.

There was a kind of triangular altar in the middle of the floor. On the other side of the altar, there was a high dais supporting an intricately carved wooden throne. And sagging in the throne was the headless, blood-covered body of a creature Percy had never seen before.

He brought his hand across his lips as partial understanding came to him. This was a temple. But who—or what—had he killed?

The head inside the bag moved once more. He had to find out! He snapped the *kibisis* open and—

He didn't have to take the head out. Understanding came to him then, complete and rounded, to the best of his capacity to understand—as the still-living and slowly-dying thing in the bag telepathically thrummed out its history. It gave him the information he wanted without reproaches and with complete objectivity. And, as he realized what he had been tricked into doing he almost fell to his knees.

In the almost nonexistent time it takes to feel a doubt or experience surprise, Percy came to know—

64

Long before Man, there had been the other mammals from which he had derived. And long before mammals, millions of years before, there had been the reptile. The reptile had eaten across the planet as herbivore and carnivore, had raced across it as thundering dinosaur and pigmy, rodent-like lizard. In a span of time beside which the reign of mammals was as a moment, the reptile had ruled the Earth with an absolute despotism in all the forms—and many more besides—that his warm-blooded successor was to achieve.

Inevitably, one of these forms laid its accent on intelligence.

A creature arose which called itself Gorgon and walked its way with pride. Great cities the Gorgons built; they captured and tamed the unintelligent dinosaurs and made cattle out of them, even to the ground-shaking Brontosaurus. Those they could not tame, they destroyed for sport, much as a thoughtful simian newly arrived from the trees was to do much later. And, partly for sport, partly for burning conviction, they destroyed themselves.

War after war, super-weapon after super-weapon, they fought and lived through. They even destroyed the continent on which they had originated, the home of most of their science and art and all of their major industry—they saw it sink into a boiling sea, and they lived through that. Then, at last, they gathered in their shrunken numbers upon inhospitable shores and created a way of life that made war between them impossible.

There was a brief season of great cooperative achievement, an instant or two of Indian Summer, before the curtain began to fall upon the Gorgons once more. Their seed had been injured by one of the latest weapons: they were no longer breeding true. In small quantities at first, the number of monsters and defectives being born increased rapidly. Almost the entire energy of the race was channeled into a frenzied biological research.

They cured every disease that had ever made them the slightest bit uncomfortable, they doubled and quadrupled their life-span again and again, they came to such ultimately complete understanding of their bodies and minds that they were well-nigh god-like and just this side of immortality. But still, every generation, there were fewer of them. . . .

65

Eventually they made peace with their approaching racial death, and set themselves to cheat it by passing their knowledge and achievements on to another creature. This was not easy to find. First, they tended to look within the ranks of the reptiles for a successor, but they had depleted the vital energies of the best nonintelligent species as badly as they had their own. They had a brief success with the serpents and pythons but, despite increased intelligence, no amount of selective breeding or indoctrination could persuade these creatures to live communally. Second, they tried the amphibians; then the birds—

After many trials and many errors, the Gorgons settled at last on the mammalian primate. Here, however, with much difficulty and heartache because of the creature's fundamentally alien orientation, they achieved success. Slowly, over the unhurried centuries, the Gorgon selected this stock, discarded that one, gently stimulated and educated, until a civilization of sorts had been achieved. A little longer and they could throw aside the mantle of godhood and teach their charges directly.

But the Olympians came.

It was true, as Hermes had told Professor Gray, that a weakness in the sub-spatial of fabric between universes had made it possible for them to enter. He had neglected to mention that they were the first and only ones to invade this universe, they and the assorted monsters, that a completely different corpus of natural law made it possible.

Originally, they poured into Earth from almost every spot on her surface. They conquered and enslaved, killed and looted, but their chief object was land. The available space on their own highly crowded world was very limited.

And there were only a handful of Gorgons to defend mankind against them. Hurriedly, these ancient reptiles turned to their forgotten and hoary armories, brought out the weapons they had sworn never to use and plunged into combat to save, not themselves—for this they were now psychologically incapable of doing through warfare—but the infant race they guarded. And slowly over the years—while liquid fire rained upon one land and floods swept through another—the invaders were driven back and the exits sealed one by one.

The Gorgon losses had been small numerically, but devastating in proportion to their total strength. There were only three females who escaped being mortally wounded; two badly crippled males had hung on for a century before dying without viable offspring. The three remaining intelligent reptiles saw no alternative but to concentrate in the Eastern Mediterranean and provide at least a section of the human race with an accelerated course of instruction.

Then, five hundred years ago, the outsiders were heard from again. This was a remnant which, cut off on this planet by the Gorgon victory, had returned to the sealed-off Mount Olympus exit and secretly rebuilt its strength. They had attacked one awful night and wiped out Cnossus, the capital city. Wearily, the Gorgons turned back to combat. They drove the Olympians off and crushed them for the time, but were no longer strong enough themselves to wipe out completely the golden-skinned race. A degenerate fragment remained which was now, like humanity's protectors, a constantly dwindling species.

Before this had been achieved, however, every large city in Crete had been gutted and Sthenno and Euryale, Medusa's sisters, had been killed. She worked desperately now at her double task: to pass on as much of the Gorgon knowledge as humanity was capable of absorbing and to rebuild enough of the ancient weapons to prevent the one remaining danger—an Olympian attempt to break through the sub-spatial fabric once more and regain contact with their parent universe.

To this end she had been preparing a multitude of weapons which men of this time, under her direction, could use against the Olympians. Unfortunately, the entire orientation of the Gorgon educational process had been opposed to war and weapons. This generation of Cretans, while superior in brains and breeding to most twentieth century humans, were decidedly not warriors and were having great difficulty developing the martial spirit.

Medusa had been sending the priestesses through whom she governed to nearby lands in search of a people who, while possessing the requisite belligerence, were sufficiently advanced intellectually so they still could be persuaded of the necessity of joining the last campaign against the Olympians.

The concept of forcing people to fight—even for themselves —was anathema to a Gorgon.

But she had been anticipated. The Olympians had evidently managed to receive some sort of message from their own world and believed that, by operating on both sides of the sub-spatial barrier, they could effect another breakthrough. It was probably one of the last attempts that could be made (possibly the civilization in the other universe was beginning to dissolve under the continual corrosion of war as the Gorgons' had), and they considered it essential to remove the last of the ancient reptiles to insure that they would not be interrupted.

Knowing that they were far too weak and backward now to carry off a frontal attack with any success, they must have developed the idea of using Percy as a catspaw. Probably, the head mused, one of their number—scouting among ordinary people for crumbs of information Medusa might have dropped—happened upon a superstitious myth-prophecy and decided to develop it into fact. The arrival of a young man from a previous space-time universe worked in perfectly, since no human of this period could be persuaded or frightened into attacking a Gorgon.

And, at the reason why a human assassin was needed by the Olympians, Percy's knees almost buckled.

For no Gorgon, my son, is capable of injuring a human being without committing immediate mental suicide. It would have been like a mother stabbing her crawling infant for me to have killed you, as I could have, when your harpe *sang at my throat.*

"Listen," he said desperately to the tired, dying head in the black bag, "you may not want to force people to fight for their world, but I don't have any such compunctions. I've certainly been forced to do enough things in my own life that I most definitely didn't like! Now, I know a place where there's a bunch of plenty belligerent characters—and I know a way of getting them to volunteer for the forward echelons. I want to do what I can to fix up this terrible thing I did!"

Medusa considered. He could feel her holding on to her vital energies with more and more difficulty, despite the enormous psychosomatic control practiced by the Gorgons. Her life was seeping away.

Yes, the faint thought came at last. *Yes, it might save the planet. It must be tried. Call Athena, young man. Call her with your voice.*

He hesitated for just a moment. He licked his lips. It would be kind of nasty if this was just another trap. "Athena!" he called.

Almost immediately, an old priestess hobbled down the hall to the balcony. She clapped her hands to her ears and her mouth distended in horror at what she saw, but at a rapidly telepathed order from Medusa, she controlled the scream in time.

This is no time for sorrow or anger. Weeping must come later in its proper time and place. Meanwhile, the Olympians prepare to tear down once more the barrier between the worlds. If they succeed, there will be none of my race to stand between them and you. They must be stopped! All else must be subordinated to that necessity. So, go, call your sisters together and make ready for the things I have prepared for this day. And hurry, Athena, hurry!

An efficient nod and the old woman had gone back down the hall calling her subordinates.

What are you going to do? the thought came.

Percy told her. There was a pause. Then, *Let it be done, then. But remember my son, no matter what the circumstances may be, I cannot injure a human being!*

Athena returned with a dozen or so wide-eyed, frightened young priestesses whom she organized and ordered so efficiently that they had no time to do more than bite their lips occasionally at the thought of what the *kibisis* contained. Even so, they made Percy feel terrible. He had killed not merely their deity, but their wise teacher and gentle friend. And why? Because he was a sucker.

Well, he was through with that from now on, he vowed. He knew what the score was—and from here on out, he would be acting on what he knew rather than on what others told him.

Each priestess was standing on a wide metallic rug piled high with shimmering weapons that looked like spears and battle-axes, but that he knew must be disguised as such merely to be credible to the people of the period. Athena beckoned and he stepped onto her rug. She pulled a tiny switch set in a corner box and turned a small wheel. The rug rose and soared from the huge balcony with no feeling of motion.

"The island of Seriphos," he said to Athena in reply to her questioning glance. Behind him, he could see the other priestesses each on her flying metal carpet strung out across the sky.

They flew over the waves at a much greater speed than he had when traveling with Hermes. This was a tremendous science he had killed, Percy thought wistfully. All these millenia of working and nurturing and along comes a stumblebum named Percy Sactrist Yuss who has listened to a good smart line and—

Had it happened the same way in his own previous spacetime universe, he wondered? Well, there was no way of knowing. Right now he was operating completely outside the framework of the legend—at least Professor Gray had told it to him. Anything could happen.

They came down directly in the village square, as Percy had intended they should for maximum effect. And, while the townsfolk stood around with mouths hanging as slack as their hands, he strode toward the palace with Athena hurrying along on his right.

"I wonder," he said, out of the corner of his mouth to the black bag. "This *harpe's* getting heavier. I can't walk with as much dignity as I'd like to. Could you try some of that hypnosis stuff, perhaps. . . ."

He strode into the pillared hall with clanking boots. He stopped against the massive column where he had been placed upon being brought to this hall as a prisoner. King Polydectes was having lunch. He rose from the long, crude wooden table at Percy's entrance and started to wipe his lips with a nearby wife's hair.

"Welcome home, Perseus, welcome home!" he said with a creaking, somewhat laborious enthusiasm. "We've been waiting for you to return!"

"Have you now?"

"Oh, certainly my boy, certainly! Ever since that tragic mistake out at the theater, we've known for certain you were

70

really Perseus. I've punished that zoo-keeper horribly, I assure you! Why, he was supposed to have a hundred dancing flower-decked maidens greet you and the girl. Somehow or other he got confused and rang in that scylla. I have absolutely no idea how he made such—"

"Can it. I'm here on business. Call everybody in who can get here fast."

Polydectes nodded vehemently and waved at Dictys with both hands. As his brother obediently sped out of the hall, the king, his eyes fastened warily on the black bag that swung at Percy's side, asked in what he evidently considered was a winning voice: "Aren't you going to say hello to your mother?"

Percy stepped back. "My—my mother?"

"Yes, she arrived this morning. When she told us her name, we realized how completely the legend had been fulfilled. We've been making her as happy as possible since, even though it has been a little—eh, a little—expensive."

He pointed to a spot halfway down the table. Percy gasped, then let it roll out into unbelieving laughter. Mrs. Danner sat in her dirty flowered housedress, her arms bent around a huge wine-skin.

"Poor little Marybelle Danner," she was mourning between slobbers. "It's all weak stuff, the best they got's like a baby's slap. And they mix it with water yet!"

So even this much of the myth was fulfilled too! Not a Danae but a Danner had arrived to be associated with him. And the fact that she wasn't really his mother? " 'She's somebody's mother, boys,' he said."

Obviously, if someone was needed to round out the generalities of a legend, they too "fell through", parchment or no parchment. Although he'd like very much to question Mrs. Danner on the exact mechanics of her arrival. It might be important and useful. . . .

"Take good care of her," he ordered. "And Dictys!"

"Yes, sir," the king's brother inquired as he reentered the hall with a substantial and highly uneasy section of the population behind him. He too kept throwing anxious glances at the *kibisis:* everyone seemed very well educated in the legend

71

on this point. "Anything I can do for you? Anything at all? Just name it, that's all I ask, just—"

"Somewhere on the southern tip of the island," Percy told him, "you'll find an old man, together with the girl who escaped from the arena with me. I want you to find them and make them as comfortable as you can. Concentrate on nothing but making life pleasant for them until I return. If you get slack anywhere along the line, you'll hear from me. Understand?"

"I'm on my way," Dictys assured him. "Hey, Menon, Bupalus, Pataikion! This way. We've to run. Favor for a hero, a man we all admire!"

Percy grinned as the three violently nodding men followed Dictys out of the hall. It was fun to unsucker. But he had business, important business, as the sight of the grim priestess at his back reminded him.

"Polydectes," he said, "you are about to start the first draft in the military history of Seriphos. I'm on my way to attack the Olympians and I'd like you to furnish about fifty good fighting men to assist me in the project."

The king stilled the crowd and turned nervously back to the young man before him. "Uh . . . my people like to stay out of other fracases. That's why they call me—"

"I know," Percy told him. "I know. Only this is urgent. I want those fifty men very badly indeed. We'll give them powerful weapons such as they've never dreamed of before—and teach them their use. But this is your chance to cut down on that surplus population you're always talking about. And, as I said, it's very important to me." He patted the *kibisis* delicately as he spoke.

"Oh, in that case," said King Polydectes. "If it's urgent! Why, certainly. Captain of the Guard! Detail all twenty-eight members of the army, the ten policemen and any twelve members of the Citizens' Reserve for duty with this famous and spectacular hero. If anyone grumbles, tell him he can choose between that and being cooked over a slow fire."

"I see you've repaired the execution pot," Percy commented.

The king shook his head unhappily. "No, it was a dead loss. And we can't get any kind of decent replacement anywhere. But we've been experimenting with barbecue recently. The results, while not perfect as yet, show a good deal of promise. I'm very hopeful."

Percy walked outside to watch the fifty men being assembled. The priestesses had broken them into very small groups and were explaining the functions of the strange new weapons to them. The men looked half-dazed and half-resentful; the fact that women were teaching them how to fight seemed especially confusing. But the presence of "the hero", and the young women's business-like approach successfully kept their attention from wandering.

The head of Medusa stirred in the open *kibisis*. *Hurry, my son. The time of my last weakness draws near.*

"One last thing," Percy assured her. He turned back to the palace entrance where Polydectes stood munching on the dripping leg of a sheep and watching the whole scene with friendly interest. I've done my part, his attitude suggested. I've given of the flower of my country. The best I have. No sacrifice can be too great. . . .

He stared from the king to the weeping women bidding their husbands and sons goodbye, the nervous male conscripts trying to understand their instructors and obviously wondering how they had gotten into a war with Olympians, and back to the chewing monarch.

"There's one thing you haven't been told," he announced. "King Polydectes has volunteered to lead his troops into combat. King Polydectes isn't afraid of the Olympians, so long as he has our weapons to use against them. King Polydectes says, 'Damn the thunderbolts, full speed ahead!' "

"I d-do?" The chunk of mutton dropped to the ground, the sound of its fall obscured by the cheer that went up.

"You most certainly do," Percy told him. He grabbed the quivering monarch with one hand, and stroking the black bag suggestively with the other, drew him gently on to the metallic rug which Athena operated. The other priestesses followed suit with their charges. "This is why," he said in a voice that echoed back and forth across the square, "they call you Brave King Polydectes!"

They took off to the accompaniment of another wildly rattling cheer.

Once they were scudding along the curve of the Greek mainland, Athena began explaining one of the weapons to the ruler of Seriphos.

"You sight your target in the holes running lengthwise through these spears—like this. See that rock? Then, as soon as you've made your sight, you press this little button in the rear. After that, all you have to do is let go of the spear. It won't miss."

"I'm an old man," Polydectes muttered. "Toothless, worn and feeble. In the bleak winter of my life, all I want to do is lie by the fire and watch the youths frolic and fight. Ah, youth, youth!"

Percy walloped his back heartily. "Well, we're giving you a new lease on life! You might as well pay attention, because when we come down, we'll come down fighting. And there's no turning back!"

They passed two great peaks near the coast. "Mount Pelion," Athena said, nodding at the first. "And that's Mount Ossa. Olympus is next."

My son, came the hurried thought. *I am dying fast. Grasp my head by the long hairy spines on its back and hold it in front of you when you attack. And, if you are about to be overcome, throw it at your enemies. But you must move rapidly! Already can I sense the dissolution of the impermanent interspace that keeps one world from disturbing another. Our enemies will pour through and overwhelm the pitiful striving. Remember your strength! Remember that it is greater now than when the false Olympian led you to the balcony of my temple in New Cnossus. Feel it, my son, feel it leap through you; feel your mightiness!*

And, as they neared the majestic mountain and swung into a circle of carpets for the attack. Percy felt the strength boil in his muscles. He wouldn't have any trouble wielding the *harpe* now!

The only trouble with that was that all of his weapons had been given to him by the Olympians. Wouldn't they know how to deal with them?

He seized a spear as a horde of golden-skinned men swirled off the side of the mountain and rose to meet them. Sighting somewhere in the center of the group, he pressed the button. The spear buzzed out of his hand and plunged down-ward, splitting three Olympians like so much *shish kebab*.

Beside him, he heard a similar noise as Polydectes let a weapon go too. The king's success was even greater—he got four flying outsiders. Now that they were in combat, Polydectes was concentrating on nothing but the kill, the most efficient kill, as befitted a barbarian monarch.

A sheet of flame flashed down from one of the carpets as someone brought another weapon into play. An entire group of ascending Olympians vanished. They turned and sought shelter in the mountain again.

Now, they had the advantage. The long, purple cone of a ray gun raked across a carpet and exploded it. Then another shattered outward. The priestesses brought their craft up higher, out of the ray gun's obvious range.

"Won't work," Polydectes told Percy crisply, as if he'd been advising him on military strategy for the past five campaigns. "They'll come up one at a time now and burn us down. Whatever this thing is that we're flying, we've got to go in after them!"

Percy nodded. He gestured to Athena who, making an overhead motion to the other priestesses, spun the little wheel rapidly. They swooped down, the fore-part of a long parabola of carpets.

Take me now, my son, came the urgent summons. Now!

Percy grabbed the lizard-like head out of the bag by a lock of something on the back that was very much like green hair and held it out in front of him. He reached around and whipped out the *harpe*.

The purple rays died out. He heard screams of terror from below. "A Gorgon, a Gorgon!"

"Yes," he said grimly. "What's left of the one you fellows talked me into killing. It's coming back to roost along with the sucker that did the job!"

They touched the ground and he leaped down, clicking his boot switches into action. With this much extra speed, he'd match a sword against a ray gun any old time!

Except that from the mouth of the immense cave halfway up the mountain a dozen golden-skinned men poured out wearing identical boots and blasting purple cones ahead of them! And they moved so much faster than he did, their boots were either better-fueled or better-made.

Polydectes behind him accounted for one of them. And a sheet of flame flapping down from one of the nearest descending carpets burned half of the rest out of existence. He ran on toward the cave desperately trying to dodge and circle around the burst-provoking rays.

One of the Olympians angled in front of him. Percy cursed, realizing he would never be able to reach him in time to use the *harpe*. The fellows's ray gun came up.

And Medusa struck.

Percy, catching her agony in his mind, realized what the effort had cost her. But the Olympian fell forward in cracking fragments; he had been completely ossified on the spot!

So another aspect of the legend was true! Medusa could—

He was inside the cave now and had no time to think. In front of him there was a rank of determined and armed Olympians, some sixty or seventy deep. And beyond them, over their heads, his eyes rapidly followed intricate whirls of wiring and shimmering instruments to where—at the rear of the cave—a little whirlpool of red energy was growing larger in the rocky ceiling.

They were breaking through! At this very moment, they were acquiring reinforcements from the dread other side!

Feverishly, he poured into the attack, slashing them from before him like so many scallion heads on the restaurant cutting board. Besides him, he could hear Polydectes roaring and the men of Seriphos as they poured up.

But he couldn't make it! He'd have to climb those Olympian-filled steps. He knew it despairingly as he hacked and dodged, slew and was ripped himself. He saw that the little whirlpool had grown larger now, that a huge machine had taken shape on the other side and was coming through.

Throw me, Percy! The Gorgon abruptly screamed in his mind.

He brought his arm back and threw the head straight at the skimming scarlet circle high overhead. There was a moment of last instruction that thrummed inside his brain, then the shrill agony of dissolution as the head touched the red energy whirlpool and exploded.

The Olympians screamed their despair when the dust had

blown aside sufficiently to show that the entrance was gone. It had been sealed again forever, Percy knew. Never again would they be able to pool their bit of half-knowledge and rebuild their side.

The men of Seriphos pressed in for the completion of the kill. A few Olympians managed to escape out of the cage mouth and soar away, but those who remained fought listlessly.

What were those last instructions the Gorgon had shot at his mind? *The poem! The poem!*

Which poem? The one beginning: *"And thence came the son of Danae, flaming with courage and spirit—"*?

He was standing on a sunny hilltop in the northern part of a small island. There was no one near him.

Percy looked around stupidly. What—

Then, as his mind settled slowly and he remembered the advice Medusa had frantically telepathed to him, he understood. He wasn't happy, but he understood.

Now that the Perseus sequence was over in that particular space-time universe, it was possible only to arrive at the beginning of the one in the next. And while the parchment was gone, the poem related to him, to Percy-Perseus. With that subjective aura and the psychological impetus the Gorgon had given him, he had only to remember the lines of the poem to be precipitated into the next universe.

Why? So that this time there would be no mistake. So that this time he would not be talked into slaying the last surviving Gorgon and removing from humanity the fountain of ancient peaceful wisdom which could nourish it. So that this time he would not—at long, long last—be a sucker.

He regretted it. He especially regretted the loss of Ann whom he had hardly come to know.

But, come to think of it, wouldn't there be another Ann Drummond in this universe? Yes, and couldn't he be even more successful? He knew his way around now. He'd do that little job for the Gorgon, all right, but first Percy—or Perseus as he might as well call himself here—was going to strut a little. He was carrying a small armory, he knew his power—and he wasn't taking any con games from any man.

No, this time Seriphos was going to hear from him right at

the start.

He started down the hill-side, not noticing the young man paddling furiously in a just-materialized bathtub out in the bay.

Nor did he notice the squad of King Polydectes' soldiers eating their uninteresting meal in a clump of bushes halfway down the hill. Nor, if he had seen them, would he have known that their commander was the type to have annoying strangers knocked out from behind so their fine clothes could be stolen at leisure.

Especially was their commander that type after a hot, irritating day spent fruitlessly chasing *harpies* in the hills by order of King Polydectes. . . .

THE END

THE PLAYERS OF HELL

Dave Van Arnam

PRELUDE: *Wizard's Dawn*

(From the *Eighth Scroll of Firanzu*)

. . . Now I, Firanzu of Mallion, being full of many great and wonderful tales, have often been accused of spinning fancies out of my bare brain, or shuffling out others' tales and bringing them back so jumbled only their maker might remember their origins. Yet I tell you all, that if I could not speak the truth I would fall silent.

And how might I fall silent, with the tales I have to tell? As for this one, in many voices, thieves, magicians, heroes, and some women, all mixed briefly together. I have other tales about them too, this being but the trifle that struck the first great chord of a secret combat . . . which comes later, I regret. But if you seek them, begin here; twist the scroll further, my masters, twist the scroll!

. . . Heaviness of night just before morning, and the wind chill. Looming—the castle.

Vast and night-ridden was the mighty castle-palace of Azeltarem, the Black Magician, in the huge shadow of the Mountain Shaiphar.

Flickering in the cavernous windows were dim torches. Outside, all was yet black, for it was The Night of No Moons.

Thus the prelude on a fateful night, my masters, as I vanish for a time into my tale.

For, inside the castle, though all was brilliant and flame-drenched, was blackness also, for congathered here on this omen-ridden night were the Spellmasters of Sezain. Workers some in good, some in evil, they were bidden by Azeltarem to attend presently at Shaiphar to share his mind. It was understood by all that certain matters of dark and mystic portent would be made clear to them, even to those who had suspected nothing before.

"The situation is too unclear. I like it not," muttered Varnashoth the Eld, of Zemna Keep. "The Black One has no cause to love or trust or aid us, nor we him. Can his pretentious omens—yes, yes, Taher, I know as well as you do—can his omens outweigh the safety of our brotherhood?"

"Ah, yes," came the low answer of Taher Kmatis, his thin drawn face abnormally white in the red flickering of the torchlit corridor. "But as for me, my own worthy lord Thranor in Kazemi waits eagerly for my return. The knowledge I may gain here, and elsewhere, will yet suffice to win me the fair maiden Riahi, in spite of my cursed brother, with—"

"With promise of Thranor's kingdom at his death; yes, yes, Kmatis, I know your old ambitions. But these bleak halls we pace house Ambition personified. Speak not of secrets; you and I, we know one deeply held within these death-grim walls—and for how long it has been kept . . ."

The two fell silent as they came to the giant entranceway to the Hall of Counseling, and adjusted their grey cowls about their heads.

Just inside the entrance to the Hall of Counseling, a giant cage of iron hung suspended from the ceiling. A dozen yammering dwarfish beings inside it gripped the bars and screeched incomprehensibly at the ominous grey figures passing near them.

Taher Kmatis shuddered.

"He jests more grimly than ever," said Varnashoth the Eld, quietly.

"The new one was Lainniat of Samand, was it not?" Kmatis glanced at his companion, who nodded.

"He attempted the spell of tarnflowers and the seldom-grass—though I warned him Azeltarem had set the Incantations of Tron upon such uses. Lainniat could not believe the Black One had such power in Tron when he does not own

80

the sigil. Ah, well." The old man with the incongruous black beard sighed.

In the Hall stood a huge semicircular table, the open half toward the two who had just entered. Beyond, a coal-black throne towered commandingly above the council table, behind which, facing the throne, sat nearly the entirety of the brotherhood of the Spellmasters of Sezain.

Though the throne itself was vacant, such was its power in their imaginations that it drew nearly everyone's eyes, and they sat almost in silence staring at it, only a hushed murmur of words dimly audible.

Some were less reverent, it was plain, for the short, powerful figure of Shagon of Goroth approached them, his bald head glistening with moisture, his hands in the sign of honorable meeting.

"Greetings, Elder of Zemna. And Taher Kmatis, you are far from Kazemi this cold night. Greetings."

The newcomers made the sign of benevolent greetings, and then answered him in kind, their voices low as his involuntarily was.

"It is a cold night with bitter cold comfort," said Shagon then, shaking his head doubtfully. "Most doubtful of all has been this word that the Black One breaks age-old custom and will not appear before us till the sun's rays flash upon the nightstone pendant above his throne of audience . . . it is an interruption of his nature that concerns me."

"It seems a fair portent to me," protested Kmatis, though one hand nevertheless rubbed nervously against the rough grey cloth of his other sleeve. "One wisely does not ever trust the Black One, but I will ever trust him less at night, among his element and source of power."

"Kmatis, when great lords change their ways, lesser ones must seek out causes, lest in ignorance they—"

Shagon interrupted tall old Varnashoth. "See, the light!" he whispered.

The Hall of Counseling was an inner hall of the shadow-haunted palace-castle of Azeltarem. Yet on the side toward the morning sun there was a tiny vertical slit in the wall, which opened onto a small anteroom whose wide tall window allowed the early sun to drench it in its green-gold rays.

The assembled Spellmasters murmured more actively among themselves, aware that it was to begin.

A thin wavering beam of light pierced through the gloom of the Hall of Counseling. Voices speaking low dropped into silence, as all looked upward.

The beam of light traced downward over the high black canopy above the throne of Azeltarem.

The beam struck the nightstone, which hung motionless above the spot a man's head would occupy, sitting on the throne—

And the beam vanished, along with every other source of light within the hall, from the torches that had been burning fiercely in their cressets to the brightfire ring on the left thumb of Varnashoth the Eld.

Then the blackness passed, and all was as before . . .

. . . save that the ray of light had now passed by the nightstone, and Azeltarem the Black Magician sat darkly in his throne of audience and power, his eyes points of black reflecting light roving restlessly over the assembled figures in grey.

At last he spoke.

It seemed his voice was but a tiny aged whisper—but it filled the room with its subtle persuasive melody.

"Vast danger roams the lands, my lords, all the New Lands, vast subtle danger that I alone have detected within the last twentyday. It is for this reason I have summoned you. A terror is rising up against us, even against us, that we in our massed powers may not be able to resist.

"It will take no heed of good or evil. It will attack us all, quiet blindly, perhaps irresistibly."

The thin voice paused as if to summon more breath into the weak aged body by an effort of will.

Taher Kmatis met the gaze of Varnashoth. The brow of the Eld was knit with consideration. Taher shot a glance at Shagon, then looked back at Varnashoth and nodded toward the powerful bald figure.

Shagon rested slumped in his oaken council chair, a thin smile on his lips, his eyes almost closed, hardly looking at the commanding figure on the high black throne.

"Odd that he should seem so casual," thought Taher. "He's seldom present when the Black One deigns to address us."

82

Varnashoth leaned toward Taher Kmatis then, and would have whispered, but the thin high music of Azeltarem's voice once more cast its master's menacing words among the multitude of Spellmasters.

"My lords, there are those of you who know I have devoted some effort to keeping the old sigils of power out of the hands of those who would misunderstand and misuse them. Some of you are even aware that the cursed Lady Tza herself has recently obtained no less a focal point of power than the Sigil of Tron. You will say, being masters of lore, that she has not the knowledge and the power to wield such a mighty artifact, no more than most of you would be.

"It is not true. How she has done it, I do not know, but I have clearly seen that she means presently to utilize the Sigil of Tron, and if she does, she will surely be unable to control it for long—its power will then flood out upon the New Lands unchecked, wreaking havoc even among you and seriously threatening my own power, deep in the mysteries of Tron and Lord Tir'u and Touraj of the God Lands of Tormitan."

Varnashoth knit his brows, the Taher Kmatis found himself heaving a giant sigh as the Black One paused again. It was not like Azeltarem to speak of the sources of his power, especially not when addressing a multitude of workers in the same flowings of natural power.

"And there are other matters that threaten, other dangers in the New Lands. We may have to meet again to summon up another surge of common strength.

"For that is what I ask for now. You must know that I have laid some small plans for obtaining the Sigil of Tron from its resting place in the Lady's Ebon Tower in Zetri—and that I cannot read the ending of the adventure."

There was an involuntary susurrus of whispered exclamations. Once more Tahar Kmatis studied Varnashoth the Eld of Zemna Keep, who turned to him, blinking rheumy eyes, and said, "At last the New Lands gain another adversary. I wonder how he and she will take to the new one . . ."

Taher felt an urge to grin, but had no desire to end up in any of Azeltarem's cages. Then he had a slight illumination in the back of his mind, and whispered back at Varnashoth, "*Is* it a new one . . .?"

"My lords," Azeltarem said, and his voice became even more penetrating; the Hall of Counseling rang with the thin, knife-keen voice. "My lords, some fear, some hate me, even among your ranks. Some . . . have cause. Others do not. Some, as I know, deem me more evil than all midnights, call me master of everything ill that runs strongest in the night."

Taher Kmatis thought, with a quick savage surge of bitterness. *He's finally going to persuade the brotherhood to help him. He'll have us doing his work in all the New Lands— when this is done we MUST have an Inner Counsel . . .*

"And indeed," Azeltarem continued, "it has been long since I shed certain scruples many of you yet hold to. Wisdom is wisdom, which is power, which is life. So spoke the ancient holders of my title since the Autarchs fell and the Emperors perished in the Old Lands, Pazatar and Armassic. The central word . . . is *power.*

"And now we shall need all our wisdom, all our power—or we may not hold life much longer. Old matters? Let them remain old, touching only . . . some of us.

"This new matter touches all of us!

"We must make alliance!"

CHAPTER ONE: *Swords at the Inn*

"As ALL GOOD STORIES DO," said the stocky man in the dim-lit tavern, stripping off his leathern jacket, "this one begins with a fight!"

"Well, then, Captain Konarr, prepare to die!" The slender young man in faded crimson and black caressed the hilt of his sword, a sneer on his almost-handsome face.

The long hot day had faded into the cool breezes of evening. Inside the Inn of the Cudgel, soldiers and tradesmen and travelers, laborers, hangers-on, servants with a free day, sat mingled together at age-darkened benches, drinking cool ales and wines.

The Inn of the Cudgel dominated the outpost village of Bephan almost as much as did the outpost camp of the Free Company that guarded it. It was Konarr's Free Company, and it guarded the Oulan Road from nomad marauders over the last forenoon's journey on the road to proud Zetri, Queen City of Tarmisorn.

For long afternoon hours in the drowsy warmth, Konarr had sat at his accustomed bench by one of the large windows, through which cool breezes wafted down from the grassy slopes of the Baragan Hills. The day before, he had begun a stretch of leave time, and he still had not decided what to do with his twentyday. Zetri? He didn't seem to feel much interested in anything. Much better to sit in the peaceful harmony of the inn . . .

As the sun set in the west beyond the distant spires and towers of Zetri, Konarr had called for food. Old Durrekal, the innkeeper, had presently brought him a large platter of fresh-roasted meat.

It was as Konarr was raising the first hunk of meat to his

mouth on the tip of his knife that the dusty, travel-stained stranger had entered.

Scarcely had the lad set foot inside the portal when a drunken offduty pikeman lurched up against him, propelled by a belligerent fellow pikeman. As the first pikeman turned after the collision, the stranger grasped the collar of the fellow's short cloak and flung him casually around in a half-arc directly at the second pikeman, who had caused the incident.

The stranger partly smiled, partly sneered, and continued on into the Inn of the Cudgel.

Konarr took a deep breath, his lungs filling with air flavored with the smell of ale and wine, and woodsmoke aromas melded with rich satisfying smells of meat and fat and fresh bread and honey. Then he exhaled and chuckled. This lad might prove to be of excellent mettle indeed! . . .

Much of his free time the captain spent chaffing and arguing here at the inn, laughing with friends and strangers alike, and sometimes fighting, all on politics and sword-metal alloys and soldiery, women, wizardry, warfare. He considered it both his recreation and his business, though, for he did not carouse and argue and brawl purely for the pleasures of conversation and fighting, wine and ale.

Half of his forty years had been spent in soldiering. And though his hair had become sparse and grey, his heavy-set frame had lost none of its toughness.

Captain for ten years of the Free Company at Bephan he had joined at twenty, holding the Oulan Road free from petty thieves and nomad raiders, he was a man constantly wary for larger political developments. Over the years he had swollen the ranks of his company from the normal fifty to over double that number. It made the caravan tolls higher, but the Oulan Road was popular nonetheless—Konarr's company kept the way safest of all those that entered Zetri.

Now, shifting airs of trouble and turmoil had begun to spread throughout all the realm of Tarmisorn from Zetri at its center. Hence Konarr was more than ordinarily interested in likely youths and veterans; he knew there were never too many men in a proper Free Company, no matter what traditions said.

The burly Free Captain smiled darkly; he had his own grimly humorous way of entering upon a possible recruitment. And here tonight had come a likely lad from clear across the New Lands, to judge by his clothes. The dust of the road on his once-brilliant crimson and black garments, however, did not mislead Konarr into judging him simply a defenseless, penniless wanderer. By the look of him, the spring in his feet and the poised attention of his manner, the lad was quite capable with the long narrow sword he carried slung at his left hip. Excellent!

The youth had reached the rough oak counter, and was grinning cheerfully at Lysai, the young serving maid. She blushed as she drew a mug of ale for the man standing beside him, then smiled at him as old Durrekal came up to him and greeted him with the sign of friendliness and service.

"I am called Tassoran," the youth said in friendly answer to Durrekal, "and I carry good coinage of Periareth. Drink, food, and lodging I need, in that order!"

Lysai brought a leathern jack of ale to him, which Tassoran drank off in three long swallows. Then he handed the empty jack back to the girl, asking for another, as the innkeeper indicated a large roast down the counter. Tassoran slapped down several coins, drew a short knife, and cut off a sizeable chunk of meat, which he then proceeded to eat while he stood there, washing down mouthfuls with more ale.

"What do you call this meat?" the lad asked of the innkeeper, chewing on one mouthful as he started to cut off another. "It tastes something like venison, something like roast phradon. And it's good."

"It is cut from the tchamber. Herds were brought down from the northern territories some twenty years ago. Most prefer its flesh to cattle; beef is no longer eaten here."

"It is said," said Tassoran, chewing for some moments on a piece of tchambar-meat before he went on, "that one who visits strange and distant lands will learn of strange matters. These cattle and tchambar, we have nothing like them in the eastern lands, and indeed I wondered not to see phradon grazing by the roads I've traveled lately . . . no matter."

Konarr grinned at the outlander manners that showed in so many ways, and decided on a rougher game to test whether they paralleled his abilities.

Tassoran finished his meat, picked up his half-empty jack

of chill brown ale, and started for a table near the Free Captain.

"Well, young fellow," Konarr addressed him, giving his own name as custom required, "and what tales from distant Periareth will you give us, for our hospitality, eh?"

He signaled to old Durrekal for more ale, who brought a pitcher from which to refill his jack.

He drank heartily of the ale, trying to scowl and then giving it up to once more grin at Tassoran, who all the while stood in perplexity at Konarr's words.

"Come, come," said Konarr, "perhaps a story, eh, of the latest antics of Hariri, your beloved, drunken lunatic ruler. Hariri the Stupid! Eh?"

And Konarr roared along with the laughter of his onlookers, playing broadly to the tradespeople and soldiers, who had watched such games of his before. Why, even that squat, ugly-looking stranger with the bald head was allowing himself a thin, cruel smile.

Konarr swallowed another draft of his ale, then returned to his quarry.

Tassoran of Periareth scowled at the laughter, and fingered the engraved hilt of his sword.

There was a pause, as the youth allowed the laughter rippling around the inn to die away.

"Master Konarr," he said then, plainly but with a hint of private relish, "I tell stories with poor art. But perhaps you know a few to regale us with."

It was Konarr's turn to be taken back a moment.

Tassoran continued, savoring the bite of his words: "I mind me of one told of the former Lady Tza, the illustrious mother and predecessor of your present ruler, or so they say. Refresh us with details, if you will be so kind. Something . . . I do not clearly recall . . . something about the seven days and seven nights she spent in a pig sty, granting her favors to the poor farmers of the countryside? Ah, Master Konarr, the ways of Tarmisorn are legend even in the eastern lands . . ."

Konarr's slow slight smile kept the onlookers from speaking though there was plainly a look of approval on the face of the bald, powerful man. "Very well," he said, "we have

88

traded insults handsomely, lad. Perhaps you would not mind, then, if I make up another story here, on the spot?

Tassoran looked about him. The Inn of the Cudgel was silent.

He could see the anticipation, save with Durrekal and Lysai, on the faces of the dozen or two onlookers, even that squat bald sneering one who sat drinking alone. They were all following the confrontation intently.

The youth shrugged. "How, then, do you begin your tale?"

Anticipating the answer he got, he casually began undoing the points of his cloak.

And Konarr stood up and told him, removing his jacket as he spoke.

Konarr laughed at the youth's quick answer. "Boldly spoken! Draw, Tassoran; I shall end this quickly!" He laughed again and wrapped his jacket round his forearm. "Ah, so young you are, and to taste wine no more, and to learn no more *manners* after today . . ."

The other's blade was drawn, and his faded cloak was already wound around his right forearm.

Before Konarr had more than closed his hand around the hilt of his own sword, Tassoran whipped his blade at him in a vicious sidewise swipe at the knee.

"Good stroke!" shouted Konarr, moving backward with the practiced grace of the professional swordsman and evading the whistling steel with ease. Instantly his sword was out.

The onlookers scrambled hastily out of their way, first in this direction, then in that, seeking safe spots from which to watch. Half a dozen had with forethought already grabbed their jacks of ale and were standing on a raised platform along the far wall of the inn. Over their shoulders loomed the great kegs wherein Durrekal the innkeeper stored his wines and excellent brews.

Konarr stepped back in with a backhand blow at Tassoran's right arm, catching instead Tassoran's own blade in its return stroke.

Sparks flew as the dull clang of metal sounded through the low-roofed tavern, over and over again, as Konarr and Tassoran slashed and parried through it from one side to the other, customers scattering from each new area. Once Konarr stepped backward, accidentally kicking a large black-and-white tomcat. Screeching in protest, the cat climbed up an age-black oaken pillar, disturbing a young devlet sleeping on the rafter. Thereafter the fight was continued to the occasional battle moans of the cat and the whistling snuffles of the devlet.

Durrekal himself was strangely calm as he stood to one side. Konarr had hesitated before starting this fight inside the venerable inn. There was a time when the aged Durrekal would have stepped forward at the first whisper of blade on scabbard, wielding the huge cudgel that gave the inn its name —and which now hung uselessly to the old man's arm, tied to his wrist by a thong.

Tassoran circled Konarr rapidly, his swordarm flicking out in intricate patterns, wielding the heavy blade as if it weighted no more than a short sword.

Konarr was content to stand in one spot, as much as possible, turning with the circling youth, handling his own heavier blade with even greater skill and ease.

They were splendidly matched fighters—the swift young Tassoran, his blade a lightning argument, and the older and slower Konarr, whose bull-strength and experience served time and again to save him from otherwise certain death.

For Tassoran was fast, surprisingly fast; and he marveled at the older man's uncanny foreknowledge of his moves.

Then Tassoran lashed in quickly with what proved to be a feint, but Konarr's unhesitating parry of the real blow caused the younger man to stagger back momentarily, slipping to one knee and grunting with the impact.

There was an involuntary groan from the audience, and the bald man in the corner paused with alemug poised before his open lips, his eyes now following the fight with unconcealed glittering intensity.

Not wishing to kill the lad, or to end the fight so quickly either, Konarr made it look as if his swift attack at the fallen figure was impeded momentarily by a low heavy bench, toppled over between them in an earlier pass between the two.

Thus it was that Tassoran fended off two apparently deadly blows while still on his knee—but before he could arise with renewed swiftness, he found the overhanging edge of another table at his own back, this one upright and roofing him away from getting up straight.

Instantly he ducked under the wide tabletop and kicked his way to the other side, his back sliding along the rough wooden floor. Sawdust was caught down the back of his neck; sawdust speckled his sweating arms. He cursed at the distracting discomfort, then ignored it.

Once on the other side of the table, he quickly rose to his feet and, in a mighty exertion, toppled over the heavy structure, almost catching Konarr's sword under it into the bargain.

It gave Tassoran the time he needed to collect his wits, and prepare to defend himself again. This Konarr, with the balding head and the beard already growing grey, was no mean opponent. Was it going to be necessary to kill him? And how well might he fare after that, in a strange land . . . ?

On the other side of the second overturned table, Konarr was happy for a chance to catch his breath. He was astonished, in his stolid way, not that the lad had managed to stay alive—for Konarr had no intention of killing him—but that he had even remained unwounded as yet. And Konarr's rough recruitment invariably included a little blooding for the prospective Free Soldier.

He was already certain that Tassoran had the mettle and the skill to make a valiant addition to his command; still, Konarr preferred to instill a valuable lesson in a man's soul about his captain's skills, before the man became his direct responsibility.

"Ha!" muttered Konarr under his breath, "and there are some tricks this faded youth has yet to learn!"

And, holding his blade low, he vaulted easily over the low edge of the overturned table.

As Konarr had expected, Tassoran took this for mistaken eagerness, and whipped his sword overhand at Konarr's unprotected skull.

But to Tassoran's surprise, as Konarr landed on his side of the table, his own sword was already slashing swiftly upward!

When the two swords struck, there was a loud discordant *clang*—and both blades fell to the floor from hands stung past endurance with the shock of that meeting.

This was not in Konarr's plan.

He had expected to disarm Tassoran with his trick but certainly not to be disarmed himself.

There was no time to scrabble on the floor for the fallen weapons. The youth in faded scarlet had instantly blocked his downseeking arm and was wrestling close in toward his throat.

For some moments the two fighters stood locked together in deadly combat, hand to hand, looking grotesquely like a pair of lovers.

Then, slowly, the immense physical strength of the older man began to bend the younger backward . . . backward till at last Tassoran broke away with a strangled cry and retched up on the floor among the sawdust, with his back against the wall.

Determined now to teach the upstart a real lesson, the angered Konarr strode forward swiftly toward the apparently stunned figure.

—And the youth was not there! Darting upward and forward from the floor, he grabbed Konarr's right foot as the older man approached, and deftly threw him off his feet.

Konarr twisted away desperately, trying to remain upright, but stumbled heavily forward against the wall and himself fell, momentarily dazed, to the floor.

His vision cloudy and his senses numb, Konarr staggered to his feet and looked about him groggily, knowing something was wrong but unable, just at that moment, to remember *what*.

He felt a sharp pain at the back of his neck; memory returned.

And he stood very still.

"Old captain," said Tassoran from behind him, very softly, "you are a dead man where you stand."

"Strike, then, and send me to the armies of the Gods," muttered Konarr stolidly.

There was a pause; he awaited the stroke.

"Never!" shouted the young man gaily, with a laugh. "Bend over, old captain, and retrieve your blade! We are engaged in matters of honor, not of tricks and slaughters and cowards' artifices!"

The point of Tassoran's sword was withdrawn from the

nape of Konarr's neck, and he felt a hand propelling him gently forward.

His foot kicked against his sword, and, his vision clearing, he reached for it eagerly, turning to face his laughing foe.

The sight he saw when he turned was a strange one indeed.

Old Durrekal had come near Tassoran during the course of the fight, and now had grasped the youth from behind, reaching out with an effortless motion and disarming him.

Then, with a gesture almost a caress, Durrekal touched the back of the lad's neck and he slumped soundlessly to the age-blackened floor.

But battle lust was surging in Konarr now, and he stroke toward the silent figure standing above the motionless body of his opponent.

"Stand aside, tapster," he growled, fully enraged. "This wretched felon has shamed me, in front of members of my own company to boot! Dash some ale in his face, and let us return to it!"

He looked about him, searching for familiar faces among the gloom of the low-ceilinged inn. The tomcat on the rafter spat at him as he looked up to locate the snuffling sound he had noticed for the first time; the devlet, upset by the commotion, and the cat upset because the devlet was upset.

He looked round the room once more. No eyes seemed eager to face his—except for the bald stranger, on his feet now and at the front of the crowd of onlookers.

The bald man stared piercingly at Konarr for a moment, smiled a wintry smile, and fixed his eye on the youth lying on the floor.

Konarr shook his head in pain, irritation, puzzlement, then —"Stand aside, I say!" he shouted at Durrekal. "This lout is mine!"

Durrekal did not move.

Howling inarticulately, Konarr charged the figure before him, intending to sweep the aged innkeeper aside and get to Tassoran . . .

CHAPTER TWO: *Sorcery at the Inn*

EVEN AS Konarr attacked, blood lust faded from his mind. Durrekal stood calmly before him, an unarmed, white-haired old man.

He stopped half a stride from the motionless figure standing there so quietly tall. Presently he heard the low *thuck* of the tip of his sword as it slipped from his hand tip-down and embedded itself in the floor.

There came a low groan from the crumpled dusty figure on the sawdust. Konarr passed a hand over his eyes then. *Curious,* he thought, how soon the *fight was over.* But he didn't really feel curious about it, not just then with his head spinning slightly.

"Innkeeper," came a harsh raspy voice like an amplified whisper, "you did well to stop the fight when you did."

It was the powerful baldheaded stranger, who had come up behind Durrekal and was now kneeling by the body of the stunned youth.

"I live here by sufferance as much as the next man," Durrekal said, turning to face the older stranger as he knelt by the younger. "A cock's brawl is one thing, a trifle of blood is little more—save when the blood gets into the eye, the mind's eye. I cannot afford to permit the captain of the Bephan garrison, protecting the Oulan Road, to commit the folly of slaughter upon a far-traveling youth on such slight grounds."

"Well spoken," said the stranger. "I am called Shagon. I come from Shassa, which lies, as you may know, not far past Periareth, six fiftydays hence. This lad here and I—unknown to me before—met in Ninashon ten days ago, and it chanced that he did me several small favors."

Konarr, suddenly weary, righted a toppled bench and sat down. No one was paying any attention to him anyway. Dur-

94

rekal and Shagon seemed engrossed with each other, and—
were they sensing their captain's odd lassitude?—the dozen
men from his command, so loud in their comments during
the fight, were quiet now. Like the even quieter Bephan vil-
lagers, they were drinking down the remnants of their wine
and ale, settling with the nervous serving girl Lysai, and making their separate ways outside to the crisp clean air of the
peaceful evening.

Tassoran started to raise himself off the floor, then
slumped back with a groan.

"I should like to repay this lad for his generous service to
me," said Shagon, and Konarr realized he had missed part of
what had happened. "Have the wench bring ale and meat for
him and for myself, in my room upstairs."

Durrekal nodded, then motioned to catch Konarr's attention.

"Come into the back," said the old man. "Let me look at
that shoulder."

Konarr was dimly astonished to notice a thin trickle of
blood running down the right side of his chest. He stood up
almost automatically and followed the innkeeper. His
thoughts—why couldn't he clear his thoughts? But it was too
much trouble even to worry . . .

"It was a matter of pressure applied to the proper spot on
your neck," Shagon repeated.

Tassoran was angry. He had felt a lancing jolt of agony
just as he was preparing to meet Konarr's attack, and had
fallen to the floor unconscious. Dimly he remembered being
helped upstairs by the bald man, who had sweated heavily
with the effort. Then, apart of a swallow of ale, and he was
gagging and spewing.

"What did that ancient beast *do* to me? Must have poisoned the meat, that's it. Or the ale."

Shagon began an explanation, but Tassoran became even
more angered.

Again Shagon attempted to explain, then shrugged. "It was
for your good," he observed rather coldly. "The captain was
fully enraged, eager for your blood. You fought him too well,
fellow."

"Too well?" Tassoran frowned and stared at Shagon. "Who are you and why do you say these things to me?"

"Ahhh. He is prepared for introductions. Excellent." Shagon's smile was chill. "It is well for you I admire the mettle of your spiritedness. We will leave it for the time at that. As for the other, you know me as Shagon of Shassa—"

"I do not know you at all," said Tassoran. "Yet I remember I heard you tell them down stairs that we met in Ninashon."

"I met you. Perhaps I should not have implied that you had met me."

Tassoran stood up. "I play few games, Shagon of Shassa, if that is the extent and right of your name. And when I do, I seek out laughing girls. Sir, I will not bandy words with you, but I will take my leave of you this moment." He turned toward the door.

"Stay, stay, lad, you are hasty. If you will be hasty, I must be hasty too. In brief, I have employment for you."

The lad turned. "You do not know my business and affairs. How can you know your task is in my trade?"

"Ah. When I came upon you at last in Ninashon, you proceeded to confirm my high estimation of your abilities as a master thief. It makes no difference from whom I learned this, nor how I learned you made your way to Zetri. What matters, is the manner in which you took but one brief evening to filch not one, but two of the finest diamonds in all the Ninashon Marches—and with a brace of waregons guarding them!"

Shagon's voice was soft, his smile placid, almost sleepy.

Tassoran blinked.

And Tassoran sat down.

It was not so much that Shagon knew he had stolen the diamonds, though the inner chambers of Nezzei's small castle were supposedly inaccessible. But it had taken months to learn of the presence of the half-legendary waregons—had Shagon been observing him all the time?

"Yes, you found out about the waregons," Shagon said, "and you obtained with some difficulty the proper kind of pitchy club, and you did this and that to the club, and you made your way inside the inner chambers, and almost didn't—"

"I almost didn't get my flint and steel out in time to light the torch before the waregons were at me," Tassoran said aloud, completing the sentence, and remembering. Remembering the waregons, all fang and claw and dry stench in the perfect darkness.

But the torch was lit and blazing in time, and the waregons, man-sized, horrible as legend, screamed hideously in the rich red firelight, and vanished, giving Tassoran just enough time to secure the two gems he sought from their difficult hiding place and get away free, before Nezzei could come stumbling in, half a dozen sleep-eyed guards fearful in his wake for their lives . . .

"And," continued Shagon relentlessly, "now that you have the diamonds safely, you can proceed to Zetri and hope you find someone in the Magicians' Quarter who, for such a price, will take the ulth-crazed, full-grown devlet from your trail, eh? And then you can see to the one who did it, eh?"

"You know too much, not to be a warlock," Tassoran stated. "I'll have naught to do with warlocks, and thank you." Again he rose to leave.

He sat down again slowly.

A ring of flame had come into being and was hissing round his head, causing sweat to pop out involuntarily.

As he touched the chair, the ring of flame winked out.

"Very well," said Shagon. His tone was colder yet, and this time rang with a strange finality that chilled Tassoran. "I have certain . . . powers, as you have now seen. I am, after all, a Spellmaster of Sezain."

Tassoran sighed and closed his eyes, then opened them resolutely after a moment.

"I do not like wizards, nor warlocks, nor even Spellmasters, Shagon of Shassa. Yet I will hear you out, for I see you wish to come to an agreement . . ."

"I will not hide that I speak of a small matter that is of some . . . weight in the affairs of the world," said Shagon, and his innate reluctance to disclose information to an ordinary man, even a master thief, was obvious. "No thief nor mage could make his way alone to it with safety, nor, once there, could he hope to return with the prize, though it is but a trifle in size."

"A tempting picture!" said Tassoran, wry smile on his lips. "I tell you, sir, you are no tradesman."

A scowl darkening his face, Shagon said, "Do not make games with me. I have more fire at my command . . ."

"You mistake me; I mean only that you do not gild your story with any vain enticing circumstances. Instead you show me the bones, expert to expert. Very illuminating. Yet what you tell me does not seem to lie in my line . . ."

"Ah; but a thief could not but be detected, if he used only skill, and I, for instance, should I venture there, would be detected directly by her, for I could not mask my power from her. But master thief *and* thaumaturge can do it, though it lie in the innermost chamber of the Ebon Tower in the center of her gardens between the Greater and the Lesser Palaces of the Lady Tza in Zetri."

"I am humbled by your high opinion of me," said Tassoran, inclining his head slightly toward the Spellmaster, "but can a mere Spellmaster match flames with *her?*"

Shagon smiled a grim smile. "You will see, my friend. I tell you this. I can match *anything* with the one who set the grown devlet on your trail. Will you ride with me to Zetri's gates, and inside them to my lodgings, while I unfold the pattern and the cloth to back our deeds—if I destroy the devlet?"

It was strong in Tassoran to refuse. He had ridden hard since Ninashon, to gain on the devlet, and from time to time the memory of the dry stench of the waregons returned, making him very restless at the thought of another inaccessible inner chamber. All in all, he wanted rest, safety, anonymity in some den in the thieves' quarter. Three fiftydays at least should pass before he'd venture out onto the streets of the other quarters.

Except for the devlet. He would have to seek aid immediately, once he reached Zetri—and here was Shagon, offering to free him immediately! No matter the task then, he would be free now! And perhaps he would even have the diamonds after it was all over—that might make it worthwhile indeed!

No matter that this little bull-like magician asked him instead to pluck a rarity from the innermost treasurehouse of the most feared woman in the New Lands!

"One stipulation," said Tassoran, making his decision and

98

surprising himself. "I cannot go forward if after you have told me your plans I do not think them sufficient. Agree to that, and I ride with you, and hear your words."

There was no smile from Shagon.

"Come," he said, "then there is no time to spare, for there is a presence of power nearby that I have just now become aware of. Therefore double reason we should stay no longer. And if we are followed . . ."

"There is the devlet to follow us," Tassoran pointed out, diffidently but without any indication he intended to let the point lie.

"The devlet has been dead since the fight. The baby devlet on the rafters sensed it, which was what was upsetting him."

And Shagon half-smiled, then.

Konarr heard Durrekal close and latch the cookroom door.

"Old man, what *happened?*" Konarr said, looking blankly around the cookroom, trying to reconstruct the last few minutes. A side of tchambar was roasting over a slow fire, sizzling and giving off rich aromas. "For one, I cannot even recall when he gave me this wound on my arm."

Durrekal took Konarr's shoulder and gently urged him into a lowbacked chair. "There was no wound," he said. "A little bit, a shred of magic, when the Other was thinking on his own matters."

"Other? Magic? Ho, innkeeper," Konarr said, rising up, anger stirring him again, "you know me well these twenty years. I have no traffick with magical matters, and I look to have none practiced on me."

"Sit down," said Durrekal.

Astonished, Konarr sat.

Durrekal paused a moment, assessing the sturdy captain's mood. "The time has come," he muttered half to himself at last, in a tongue strange to the other.

"Wizards' talk, by Tholk!" said Konarr, with sour-bitter realization. "I have been entrapped." He sighed deeply, wishing for a last draught of ale, then said, resignedly, "finish your spell, then, magician. I had always thought you an honest man."

Unexpectedly the whitehaired figure before him threw back his head—and laughed heartily.

"A kind of wizardry, perhaps," he said, smiles in his voice, and warmth. "Observe—but do not fear! There is no time to explain, but I mean no harm to you!"

And Durrekal made a casual gesture with his hand, as if he were casting dust.

It took a moment for Konarr to realize what was happening.

First there was a slight mistiness in the air of the closed room; it swirled, and gathered itself together in a smooth flowing. Green glitters spangled the air, and Konarr felt his hair tingling.

Then there were two figures in misty green, seated on nothingness, in the middle of the room, halfway between floor and ceiling.

Echoing voices filled the room till Durrekal frowned and made another gesture.

"—Must have poisoned the meat, that's it. Or the ale," came Tassoran's voice into the cookroom.

Konarr blinked.

"It was for your good. The captain was fully enraged, eager for your blood. You fought him too well, fellow . . ."

And that was Shagon's voice in answer; Konarr had heard it during the day. The harsh whisper was unmistakable.

Then Shagon's words changed in his mind from words to meanings, and he started to protest to the old man, to argue, to shout if necessary.

"Quiet," said Durrekal shortly. "Listen. I will explain."

"What did they mean by a *full-grown* devlet," Konarr asked, as Shagon finished talking and the two figures prepared to leave. "I did not know devlets were more than kittenlike playthings."

"They come from islands between the Old and New Lands," said Durrekal, "and in time they grow very large indeed."

Konarr scowled at Durrekal.

Imperturbably the old man observed the two figures as they made their way out of the evanescent room, then waved his hand.

The thin green mist filled the room suddenly, as if sprayed

out in all directions from the smoky simulacra who spoke from high in the air of the real room.

Once more Konarr blinked, then growled, "You should not do that, Spellmaster."

Durrekal cast a sharp glance at Konarr. "Do not call me a Spellmaster, captain, if you will. You have just seen and heard a true and current Spellmaster, speaking as if he were with us here in flesh instead of in smoke of the seldomgrass. As to its being wrong to use magic when one needs aid, captain, there are arguments of great subtlety on both sides of that question, as you no doubt know. Will you judge by results?"

Konarr frowned. "I do not know. What is your explanation for all this?"

"I cannot tell you all, for as yet I do not know it. But as I trust you, by the twenty years I've seen you, so you must trust me, for you know I have wronged no man in that time. I will tell you what I know, insofar as I know you will believe it. The rest, which strains to reach inconceivable limits of the possible, and which I myself only surmise, must ripen in its own hour or year. Begin with this: I need your help."

"What evil would you hire me to perform?" Konarr pitched his words and tone deliberately to be offensive—if he were lying, the old villain might show it if provoked, for he might well be up to no more good than that wizard above-stairs they'd watched in seldomsmoke.

"I am no wizard, though I have some . . . powers," said Durrekal. "Years ago I sought the peaceful retirement of old age; my chosen exile was to live here, where I was content to live as an aging innkeeper and to spend my days listening to the idle gossip and the travelers' tales.

"But power seeks power, and I have had of late some certain intimations that a new threat looms, to me and to all of you. Already I have heard and felt the darkness of these forces and their deeper intent, though as I said much is yet unclear.

"This is clear: the time has come to fight!"

Konarr observed the old man's merry face in total puzzlement. It was clear that the old fellow was hiding some surprise from him that presently he meant to reveal, but when would he get to it?

The aged innkeeper assumed a slightly more serious mien. "I do you ill," he said, "to play with you like this. Observe again—and once more do not fear!"

And as Konarr drew one deep breath, the wizened face before him smoothed, filled, fleshed itself out, deepened its color . . . until the face was that of a man in his early thirties!

The bent figure straightened, filled out, seemed to charge itself with some supernal energy, once more making Konarr's hair tingle . . .

. . . and a sturdy fighting man, taller by a head than Konarr, of unfamiliar land and lineage, stood before Konarr. His black hair accented the strong planes of his face, whose natural strength was not handsome, but commanding.

The tense, powerful figure of the stranger swayed for a moment. The man looked for a bench and sat down, exhaling a tortured breath and gasping for more air.

"Transformation takes a lot of strength out of me," he said after a time in a low, but vibrantly strong voice. Then he grinned in a manner oddly reminiscent of old Durrekal.

"What . . . what . . ." Konarr realized he had been babbling, and made himself keep quiet.

"I am called Zantain," said the black-haired man, more to give Konarr something to hang on to than to be informative. "I told you I have certain . . . powers. One of them is that of disguise, such as that of the old innkeeper—for now you see me as I naturally am, though I am older than I look."

"Ha!" said Konarr. "If you are older than you look, then I do not see you as you are!" His face showed his sudden glow of quick easy triumph.

"Save by devices such as disguise," said Zantain, shaking his head, "I have never appeared older than I do now."

Konarr narrowed his eyes at that. "Then you can be no other than one of the Longlived, ser Zantain." He did not go on to point out that the Longlived generally were not the well thought of. There had been eight Tzas since the founding of the Queen's Quarter in Zetri—which was almost two thousand years ago. And far to the east were rumored to be many Longlived men who passed their evil inheritances also through the millennia . . . no, it was not necessary to say more about the Longlived.

Again, Zantain shook his head. "I have lived long, but I am not of those hell lines."

A deep sigh emerged from Konarr; he was surprised and a trifle alarmed to find himself immersed in self-pity. "What can I make of it? I am only a poor captain of a Free Company; as you say, we have known each other for twenty years. I am deep in none of this lore, whoever—or whatever —you are."

"Then," said Zantain, allowing coldness to enter his tone for the first time, "you will not hear me out?"

"You would only spin me a long tale that will mean nothing to me, save that my losing my life will probably occur in it somewhere."

"My tale would be short."

"Indeed?"

"Fights. Adventure. Certainly excitement. Perhaps a little glory, after a while, if you live . . ."

Konarr laughed out loud at that, in spite of himself. "No wizard would talk like that!" he said, chuckling. "You speak too honestly for that; their works are always full of deep policy and indirection, hidden like a Dark Lord with no moons at midnight."

"Oh, there is indirection, captain. You saw and heard good Shagon of Shassa enlist our young friend who says he is from Periareth."

That made Konarr take a closer look at Zantain. "You noticed too, eh? You are far traveled for an old—well, never mind. At any rate, Tassoran may be a master thief, but he knows little of Periareth."

"Hariri the Stupid, indeed, good captain," said Zantain, smiling. "You took your life in your hands insulting Lord Hariri to one who called himself a landsman of that king."

Konarr shot a glance at Zantain. "That he did not launch himself at me with his bare hands only proved my suspicions correct. Wearing scarlet and black when the Periari believe scarlet, as the color of blood itself, is the vilest of ill omens . . ."

He shook his head as he looked at Zantain, and now they grinned together, recognizing each in the other, now, a man whose thoughts ran along similar paths.

"I will listen further to you," said Konarr at last, with still

103

a little reluctance left in him. The chance he might yet be tricked into some foolish wizardly plot dooming him to some hideous death lurked as a wordless suspicion deep inside him.

"Good," said Zantain. "The plan is simple, as I said. First, we must follow Shagon and Tassoran to Zetri and inside the gates, or rather you must; I must follow after in some few days. You must learn where they lodge and take care of certain other matters I will detail at greater length later. You will note whom they speak to, you must follow their routes through the city, you must know everything they do, no matter what they do or where they go, till I arrive."

Konarr began to protest, but Zantain went on.

"I cannot go with you at this moment because I cannot maintain my strength as myself, yet. Living as a weak old man has left me weak indeed. Further, I must arrange matters here so that no suspicious inquirers after any of us in these affairs will find aught to help them . . . You will have to disguise yourself to some extent, and you will work some magic, with my aid. But no deep magic till I arrive in Zetri and we meet to consider these events further."

"How are we to meet," protested Konarr, "if we know not where they lodge and hence cannot pick a lodging for ourselves before we arrive? You will not know where I am, and I cannot certainly meet you at a given spot at a given time, for I may be hot at their trail and unable to break away for you. You understand," Konarr said, suddenly dropping that line of argument, "I pick only one of several problems that seem unlikely easily to be solved. And then too, what is the final result to be?"

Zantain nodded.

"You will do, yes, do very well indeed, Captain. I will satisfy you on all these matters before you start. As for meeting, have you never seen nor heard of these?"

Zantain reached into a tiny wooden cupboard, recessed in the wall of the room, which popped open when he passed his hand in front of it.

From within the cupboard, he drew two tiny dull pieces of what appeared to be metal. They lay side by side and almost touched each other as they lay in his hand.

Konarr stared. "Firewasps!" he exclaimed. "I have not seen the like in ten years! Master Zantain, you are eager in-

deed that we make prompt and proper rendezvous in the
Queen City. Are you sure you will be prepared, and strong
enough, in time?"

"I must," said Zantain, with a quiet smile. "Now to some
of the problems you and I may encounter, and their various
proper solutions . . ."

INTERLUDE: From *The Scroll of Firanzu*

. . . Now I, Firanzu, must tell you of a legend that is old in Tarmisorn, and some of the truth and the error of it. And even I, once scribe to the Lady, know not all the truth of the legend, which is mightily common amongst tradespeople of Zetri and the nomads of the land both; and other such folk of like degree have much credence in such tales likewise. Twist the scroll and see, my masters . . .

Now the legend says that the first Tza, in the years after she came into the land of Tarmisorn and made Zetri the Queen City of that land, that she builded herself a great palace in Zetri city, which the like had not been seen in the thousands of unknown years there had been a settlement here. And this palace was all of white marble without stain —for this was almost full two thousand years ago, when the ancient quarries at Phalamond yet yielded goodly unstained stone.

And the Lady Tza bounded the palace with Stroams and a great lake wherein were set every kind of finned and squirming monster of the Ocean, as, the thousand-armed gaphalon from the waters of the Sea of Cheg, by the lands of Ank and Oan where men first landed in the New Lands millennia before, in the days when that which happened to Pazatar and to Armassic, happened. And in another section of the lake swam the virionne that swallows the man and the shark alike as one mouthful for his sharp-fanged jaws; and there were in another section the deadly fishes called the kannaq, whom no man has seen slaying its prey, but from whom, prey is never known to escape.

And the legend says that the spires of her palace arose a thousand times the height of a man into the sky, and were much hidden in clouds. And furthermore there was a great

106

central spire, that was builded as great around at the base as two of Tza's lesser palaces in other cities of her realm of Tarmisorn, as Pashki'oth and ah'Kluz in the north, and shadowed Malkhi itself. And the heights of this tower were never free of clouds, toward the uttermost extremity, save at the very moment of sunrise, and of sunset.

Then the legend holds that Tza did then by fearsome magicks travel to the topmost tip of her great white tower, from her star-bright throne within the Great Palace. And from the high peak and platform of that tower, they do say she hurled a shattering thunderbolt unnaturally at the very sun itself; which others do say she did as part of an immense schema of deepest magick to encapture the powers of the sky and sun for herself.

And every day she did this, morning, evening, but this endeavor continued only through the length of the first year of the Great Palace.

For on the first day after the first year was passed, since the final stone was set in the pathway through her gardens from tower to palace, in the first hour of that day, after she had cast the lightning bolt at the risen sun, there came a great greying darkness over the sky, all quietly, and the earth itself was felt to shudder, and the live hint of rain tensed the air.

But all was most unseeming quiet; and it was said that Tza herself in her greater throneroom of ivory and onyx and gemmed metals, and seated at audience on her star-bright throne, did suffer great fear, which all about her could sense as easily as they could the growing darkness outside.

And those who stood at audience with the Lady Tza that morning could not help themselves, but ran outside to the great courtyard and garden of the palace, wherein were everyone of the kinds of stones inlaid, both gentle and precious, and every kind of tree and plant did grow there save deadly herbs and vines.

And the sky grew black as a great prison, with no glimmer or chink of light in the sky, and this continued for one hour, and all the people of the city of Zetri, and of the whole land of Tarmisorn, did gather outside their homes, in Malkhi as in Kulsheth, and gazed in fear at terror above them.

Then after an hour there came a break in the clouds, and all the people of the land did gasp in awe, for it was but a tiny gap in the very peak of the heavens; yet from it poured a dazzling light, greater than any man had ever seen before or, it is said, has since.

And this light made its way downward in a thin blinding beam toward the Great Palace of Tza in her proud Queen City. And for a moment it touched the great white central tower, which stood in the beam and reflected it far and wide with its gleaming marble walls—and then the darkness was gone, at once, and the beam of light was no more.

But out of the clear sky now came the most awesome portent of all, tells the legend, which says that, from the sun itself, now halfway to its zenith—came a *black* bolt of lightning.

It struck all in a moment at the great tower, and the people of the land were blinded for a time, whether they were watching or not.

And when sight at last came back, the tower still stood; and all the people in the land were still unhurt, even to Tza herself; and Tza, they say, was mortally silent when she looked toward her proud tower of magic.

For it had turned to the blackness of that awefull mid-day night that no man ever forgot who had seen it; and that tower still stands, black as crime, and Tza never challenged the magic of the sun from that day on, though the tower still stands wrapt in clouds save at sunrise and sundown, catching as always the first and last rays of the sun; but Tza was evil as night, they whisper in versions that come from many leagues away, and found many other polluted powers of magic to enslave the land of Tarmisorn, taxing endlessly for her delights of black gossamer.

And I, Firanzu, do live now in a distant land from Tarmisorn, to tell my tales, and I tell, of this one, that I saw Zetri and lived the greatest part of my life there, and I saw there spires not much taller than in other likely cities—save for the Ebon Tower in the center of the Queen's Quarter, and even that spans not much more than twice the height of the tallest of the other towers.

The sun shines on the Ebon Tower freely, for clouds, when

they come, must come so close to ground to hide the Ebon Tower that it would be a great fog in the whole city.

Yet the legend saith otherwise, and I am loathe to doubt a legend.

CHAPTER THREE: *Thief Time in the Grand Marketplace*

TASSORAN strode through the narrow streets of the Thieves' Quarter of Zetri, toward the vast central marketplace of the city.

Much as similar congeries in other large cities Tassoran had visited in his brief life, this felons' warren seemed almost unpopulated, especially during the day. The bronze cleats on the bottom of his leathern boots clacked lonely echoes in the silent streets.

An occasional quiet burst of laughter from a window here, a whiff of oddly pleasant smoke from another, an occasional silent figure who would usually dart along another street rather than face another . . . sane sober folk from the other quarters of the city seldom liked to visit such places, even for the quietly dangerous excitement. The endless silent strangeness of it strained civilized nerves more than a few pegs past unbearable tension . . . which left thieves to themselves, and to the hunters.

But Tassoran had lived in such surroundings since he was seven years old; their eeriness to him was a tonic of normality.

He was eager to reach the central marketplace, by reputation the largest in the New Lands. For two days Shagon had been making incantations over him, and filling him with nauseating potions, medicaments, and vilely stupefying narcotics. This morning he had been weak from it, but insisted that, even though he knew the plan now, and trusted it, it was needful that he go about the city and study the nature of things. What he first wanted was fresh air, and next, to get away from Shagon.

Shagon had been irritated, but Tassoran had insisted. And

since it was, after all, a fact that Tassoran did prefer to scout in this fashion, Shagon gave in with an ill grace.

A distant dim hubbub and steady clamor became noticeable; he was almost to the marketplace, and feeling better than he had since they had arrived at their lodgings in Zetri —when Shagon had immediately begun him on a series of pasty stinking messes of weeds and other things Shagon would not name, as he stirred them in and made him eat . . .

There was a distant skirling, and a piping of horns in a merry light tune—players for a few coins in the marketplace!

He smiled, fell in step with the distant melody, and attempted to counterpoint it with his own whistling, filled with delight.

Only a thief, in very truth, could have the time to take his leisure at a time when all else who lived must needs be up and working!

Round one corner, and the tune was louder; round the next, and there was the central marketplace of Zetri itself, spread out before him in a multi-sensed tapestry of sounds and smells and colors, a shout of pure existence that suffused the young thief with a moment of pure joy.

Three musicians stood by the tented store of a spice dealer —a white-skinned lad of ten beating happily on a gnar-skin drum, a youth of fourteen with glistening coal-black skin who pumped wheezing skirls from a gross bag of winds he pumped from his own lungs, and a fellow about Tassoran's own age playing the dancing tune itself on a strange gnarled metal horn.

About them stood a half-dozen wanderers to Zetri from distant lands. As the players came to an end in their music, grinning and sweating, the visitors tossed coins to them according to their pleasure.

Tassoran reached in his pouch and scattered a fistful of coins at the feet of the musicians, who fell to their knees scrabbling for the coins with shouts of laughter.

"Ai—ai—ai! Most noble one," said the youngest, pausing in his frantic scramble, "thanks to you from Habu and Chamon and Vallasz Venai, good sir, most humble thanks!" And he dove back into the clouds of dust that rose.

"If I meet you again, and you play as well," shouted Tas-

soran over the little group's laughter, "look for like gratitude!"

And he turned and strode onto the Thieves' Wideway, the
major pathway in this sector through the tents and more permanent constructions, strode past the tented stores of the
great central marketplace of Zetri, and laughed aloud when
behind him, raggedly now, the music began again!

Coming as he had from the Thieves' Quarter, he found
himself in the least impressive section of the marketplace.
The clumps of people who dared the notoriety of the neighborhood seemed pallid and depressing to Tassoran, especially
since it was well known to all that the most disreputable purchases could here be made with great ease, albeit much
money.

This was not much to Tassoran's taste as destination, as he
was still young and without deep interest in civilized perver-
sions, sexual, emotional, physical—least of all in escapist
potions. He'd had enough of that from Shagon's magical constructions to hold him till his hair turned grey. He had pride in
his work, and remained content with wine or ale with a meal,
and enough to fill his pipe a few times afterward, then talk
with some friends, or a night's work, and a free wench from
serving quarters somewhere—that was enough for a rich full
life!

So he walked through the westernmost portion of the market seldom pausing, though he felt no need to hurry.

Once he paused to test a number of throwing-daggers, set
up in racks for customer convenience. Several seemed to his
liking, but finally he brought out his own, hefted it, and sent
its point straight into the dab of tar that was the target on the
thick plank between two tents.

Shaking his head at the knife dealer, who had no tongue
but spoke rapidly with his fingers in the manner of the
Xib'on tribesman, he went on his way.

The sun was an hour past zenith when Tassoran approached a large number of tents, from each of which ema-
nated the enticing aroma of good food.

Racks of spitted, roasted fowl on every side jutted out into
the pathways between the rows of tents. He had drifted away
from the major pattern of wideways through the market for
just this purpose.

On open grilles fresh chops were thrown for eager wanderers through the market mazes. Beside each three or four tents were other larger tents protecting rows of benches, where one could pause to eat one's purchases without paying to sit down.

Casks of clear water stood at hand also within such tents, free and subsidized by the nearby merchants.

Occasionally too there were larger, semipermanent structures, long-established taverns, well-known and expensive, though tents were the predominant structure throughout the part of the market he had seen so far.

For millennia the nomads and wandering tradesmen had come here to this spot, near the river Zasho, before the town that then was Zetri had become great with the advent of the first Lady Tza. They would set up their wares at whatever likely spot they might obtain, and remain until they had sold all of whatever they had.

Then they would strike their tents and move back to their wandering life, or over to the next trade market where they could profit from further barterings.

And when Zetri became a great town, and trade transformed its face and size and gave it a kind of majesty, still the nomads and the wandering traders returned.

Once all the square was grassy emptiness beyond the old walls; then came the nomad traders and made camp there.

Eventually the market place came into being as such, shortly before the advent of the Lady, and the walls were rebuilt to surround the trading area, now irregularly paved over. This was the sign of a major change in the market, for now many nomads ceased their wanderings for greater and greater lengths of time, desiring to trade from a fixed spot to which they began to lay genuine claim to. By laws of Zetri at that time, paving open land generally confirmed tenancy.

Then came the first Lady Tza, first of the eight, who wrapt the great mountain Chaln that had loomed beyond the new walls and marketplace, wrapt the great mountain in strange and evil spells, till it vanished forever from the New Lands; and on that spot the Lady built her palaces and towers of the Queen's Quarter.

Tassoran knew enough of this magic-haunted history to realize that he was still on the outskirts of the older marketplace proper, for as one neared the center of the market, the structures—held in family and clan hands unchanged for countless years—the structures became more and more permanent.

Tassoran stopped in front of a tent from which tantalizing aromas rolled out in an almost tangible cloud.

"Exotic morsels from Far Kazemi and the keepland marches, fair sir," said a tall stout woman dressed in a mixture of outland garbs, colorful but meaningless.

"Is your price reasonable for a good thick cut of roast groundpig?" Tassoran asked cheerfully. He really didn't care how much it cost, today.

"Do you have coin of Zetri?" asked the woman. "A scut will do it—that's the small copper piece."

"My coin is all of Periareth," responded Tassoran. "Yet I think this metal is as good as that stamped with the Ebon Tower." And he drew out a handful of copper and silver coins.

The woman plucked out a slightly larger copper piece than he had expected her to choose, and he frowned.

Catching his frown, the woman added, "Coin of Periareth, held by a man not of Periareth. Young sir, it is a mystery to me. Perhaps it might be a mystery worth solving, should a Hawk Guard of the Lady pass near by . . ."

"I have no fear that guardsmen seek me, woman," Tassoran said, then suddenly realized what she must have meant. It might be important to know the common folk were this sharp here. "Why do you call my land in question?"

"Why, you wear scarlet cloth, though it is faded with your wanderings, young sir. Never did man—nor woman neither —of that land wear scarlet on their person, for it is a doomful thing to wear the sign of blood and death . . ."

Tassoran said nothing, but his smile slowly faded.

The woman had pocketed the copper coin, and had placed a fresh-cut slab of roast groundpig on a brazier to char one side more fully, in the Kazemi manner.

"Yes, lad, I'd either change that garb you are so happy to affect," the woman said, deftly picking the sizzling meat up with the point of a sharp knife, and depositing it on a worn but clean platter of unornamented wood. "Oh, yes, indeed,"

114

she chattered on, "change the clothes, or see to changing the money, with some discreet gentleman."

It was now almost irritating to be held here by this woman lecturing him on his costume and his coinage, but he was held there first by one thought, and then by several others that came to him as he questioned the woman.

"I speak frankly to you, woman, as you have to me. How is it that no one made mention of these curious anomalies to me before, along my journeyings?"

"Periareth is a distant land and not much traded with by other lands and peoples, good young sir, which I do not doubt is why it occurred to you one day to pick it. But even a clever young Kazemi owes it to himself to study that on which he wishes to base his deceptions. No doubt there have been a silent few, a very few, who saw through your poor veilings—but rest easy, most could not have known."

"I will not hide that this thought causes me some concern, nonetheless, good mother," Tassoran said, partly falling into the Kazemi mode of address when he saw that secret too was known.

"I would not have mentioned it, fair youth," said the woman, adapting the stiff clipped accent of Kazemi with some difficulty, "had I no remedy to propose. You might speak with Chaniven Dzar. He is not a kinsman of mine nor a landsman of ours," she added hastily, seeing his protest about to break out in words. "He is not a very good man at all, perhaps, but he is fair to those he thinks he must be fair to. You will find him where this path meets the Magicians' Wideway."

"Why do you tell me this?" he asked directly, more curious than suspicious.

"I have not seen a fair Kazemi youth in many years, lad," said the stout woman, with a rueful grin. "Why I live in this troubled land I do not know, but the simplest fact is that I am far from home and likely to remain here till my square of earth is cleared and hollowed for my body. I like your face, young sir, and your adacity, and you should not carry coins of Periareth when you're dressed in blood . . ."

Tassoran laughed. "Good mother, thanks for your warm counsel. He reached for the woman's hand, kissed it with a flourish of his cap in his free hand, then let go the now blushing woman's hand, picked up the wooden platter with the slab of roast groundpig, and looked about for one of the free tents.

Chaniven Dzar bore an uncanny resemblance to Nezzei, that castled lord of the Ninashon Marches whose current reknown in the near lands was that he was the *former* owner of the two finest diamonds in the Marches. Tassoran regretted the stout woman's advice, at the same time he realized he was merely starting at phantasms.

Besides, it was part of the price to pay for being a thief by trade—that one must at times deal honestly with honest men, a great strain on your true thief, as Tassoran not only knew, but believed.

The irony that gripped was in selling a handful of outland coins, filched by hunger's necessity from a true Periari, to a man who so closely resembled the lord whose gems were presently sewn with great care inside the leathern buckle of his swordbelt . . .

"Periareth? They are true in their alloys and meltings there. Let me see . . ." Chaniven Dzar took several coins, seemingly at random, and squinted at them up close. He bit one, examining the dent with sour satisfaction, and set several others on a small balance tray for weighing.

Presently Chainven Dzan smiled slightly.

"They are good coins. In service to a family from thence, eh? They were good masters, were they?"

"Excellent and gentle," said Tassoran, "and what are the names and values of the coins of Zetri you are going to render me?"

Chaniven Dzan widened his smile a trifle. "We have coins of only two metals in Zetri, silver, a half-silver alloy, and copper. The large silver coin is standardweight, in the measure common in the lands set west of the High Mountains. The large copper coin is likewise a standardweight of copper. The other coins explain themselves. From highest value down, they are in sequence of the orders of nobility in this land, as, a queen, the large silver coin; a consort is the small. You will know them by the insignia on the obverse, and by the traditional Xalis numbering on the reverse . . ."

During the lecture, Tassoran inclined his head courteously

to Chanivan Dzan, and did not inquire into the details of the transformation of fifteen large silver coins of Periareth to ten large silver coins of Zetri, and the like percentages with his other coins. It was to be expected, since, as they both seemed to know, how could Tassoran have been in the employ of Periarthi and still affect to wear scarlet?

There was a clamor from outside Chanivan Dzan's tent, where others who desired to do business with the changer stood impatiently. Tassoran nodded again and departed.

"A fair dealer for such as I," he thought to himself, "but he looks too much like Nezzei for me to wish myself frequently in sight of him . . ."

Now Tassoran strode along the crowded Magicians' Wideway, allowing the motion of the clamoring throngs to dictate his movements here and there.

This was one of the half dozen major Wideways, but Tassoran realized quickly that it was really quite misnamed. For there were gathered only lesser workmen in the trying arts, mere journeymen of wonder, apprentices to mysteries so far beyond them that they were content to stop here and vend their tiny foolish wares.

Here were dark-visaged lads casting clouds of dust into the air, for goggling countryfolk to marvel at the resulting momentary vision of some lovely face.

Tassoran, himself possessing no hidden lore save for that pressed on him in the last two days by Shagon (and save for an old and probably useless amulet that he had carried since he was ten), was yet well aware that true masters of the art of casting dust could hold the dust picture motionless for as long as needful. Not only that, but he had heard the deepest masters could actually conjure the dread aspects of the future.

Here among the multitudes in the square were the proud, blue-turbaned tiKhaz tribesmen, none less than six and a half feet tall. In the way of the tiKhaz no youth may live who has reached his seventeenth year and is not that tall, and the maidens must be six feet at that time.

Tassoran wondered, as he had fruitlessly many times before, just what were the mysterious ways in which the tiKhaz went about disposing of the mis-sized members of their blood.

There seemed an infinite variety of people and dress. Here

and there a few times he even caught sight of an occasional Spellmaster of Sezain. Briefly he wondered how much he really knew about his temporary master Shagon's hideous brotherhood's involvement in the morrow eve's events.

Perfumes from Yush and Ophni and Sazinor filled the air, as a half dozen sweating apelike half-men of Mevorthim bearing a silken-covered litter riotous with rich flower colors came trotting through the crowds, grunting harshly on every fifth cadence to warn those ahead that a high lady of the Queen's Quarters was approaching.

Even the grey-cowled Spellmaster whom Tassoran had seen, some moments earlier, had stepped aside for the litter, forcing those near him into desperate pushings and shovings to keep from touching *his* ominous grey robe.

Tassoran had never believed the stories of the Mevorthim half-men, but when a clumsy bystander tripped forward into the litter's path, the fifth half-man turned out to be the epitome of his kind. For in one savage slash he opened the man's stomach full open with a stone knife, then ripped out the man's throat with his teeth.

The half-man worried at the dead man's throat for a moment, then cast the body aside as the fifth-cadence grunt came round with a harsh whoosh. Moments later he was back at his odd-man position helping with the litter-bearing, and the group trotted steadily away, among a ripple of silence along the Magicians' Wideway.

With some reluctance the crowd reformed in a sprawl over the wideway, though the bleeding hulk was avoided.

Tassoran stood transfixed for minutes, till the arrival of a Hawk Guard and two naked prisoners to carry off the body and dispose of it.

Did he seriously intend to walk through the halls of the palace of the woman who ruled this land and who was responsible for *that*?

Stolidly the naked prisoners hoisted the body, dripping with blood, and turned to disappear into the crowd at a command of the Hawk Guard.

Tassoran realized he was not able to think useful thoughts on his project at the time, and went on, reluctantly, till the Magicians' Wideway crossed the Jewelers', shortly thereafter.

Eagerly he turned to take the new route, hardly realizing

where he was but happy to be removed from magicians once more.

Along the Jewelers' Way at regular intervals stood posted guards, armed with crossbows which—so Shagon had warned him that morning—had been charmed at the hand of the eighth Lady Tza herself, the charm to be that the crossbows should work without mechanical fault.

It was a sensible precaution, crossbows being what they were, especially when they were guarding tents filled with riches garnered from all the New Lands.

Here were displayed precious and semiprecious gems and stones, both natural and worked in cunning fashion. Necklaces and bracelets, rings and brooches and tiaras, boxes of unworked rubies, and sacks of topaz, heaps of pearls—and solemn-faced guardsmen, crossbolts ready, sun glinting on plain steel cuirasses and shimmering on the bronze hawk helmets of the Lady's Guards.

There was no temptation here for a wary lad eager to remain a free master thief!

Not that he did not gain, for as he passed through the byways, conversing here, arguing here, discussing elsewhere, he learned that, perhaps here at the sign of the Emerald Towers, or there at the sign of the golden Road, a man with valuable secrets, such as diamonds, could find himself in potentially excellent circumstances. . . .

But—there was Shagon's plan. Failure or success, it meant there would be small likelihood Tassoran could soon show face again in Zetri. And then too, the devlet was gone—if he could trust Shagon, but there had been no signs of the monster—so there was no need to hurry the transaction.

A sound of distant horn, a drumming and skirling, broke into Tassoran's reflections on his trade and future, and he looked around to see that he had drifted to another block of shops hawking foods plain and exotic.

At some distance was a tented tavern, in front of which stood the same three musical fellows that had welcomed Tassoran to the marketplace hours earlier.

He shrugged his troubles away and made cheerfully for the tavern.

In the open flap of the tent appeared a girl.

"Away," she commanded the three musicians. "Master

says, 'Iala, we have no customers because that squalling drives them away before they dare to enter!' Away with you then, and let honest people do their honest work!'

The three stood their ground. But Tassoran could tell that they would have to give way, it being the custom in market-places that those with no tent must not remain by one whose owner objected, whatever his reason. Obviously the custom was held to in Zetri.

As Tassoran came up to them unnoticed, the ten-year-old signed, and started to pick up his gnar-skin drum. *Habu, had his name been?* wondered Tassoran.

"Hold, there, lass," Tassoran shouted. "I crave some strong chill ale and perhaps some food with it, and I am most contented in my eating and my drinking if music be played nearby. Let them remain, if you would please me."

Unexpectedly the girl scowled at him darkly a moment, giving her prettiness a new sly gamine charm.

Then she looked closer at him, while the musicians nudged each other; everyone was silent for a moment.

Tassoran laughed, and jingled his purse. The girl Iala started. "Come, come," he said, still laughing, "let us inside and to it, eh?"

He reached in his purse and tossed the drummer a large copper coin, by its markings worth a dozen tunes. "Music, lads!"

Nothing loathe, well remembering their man's generosity from earlier in the day, they struck up the tune he had liked so well then.

He laughed and entered the cool gloom of the tent, to find himself face to face with the girl.

He looked down at the pert face, noting the flash of almost animal intensity hiding in her pale blue eyes and the odd cut of her hair, as golden as his own.

She was beautiful, with a strange smile that intrigued as it puzzled him.

At least it wasn't puzzling that he intended to spend a few hours at the least in this cool tent, with those blue eyes flashing at him, and many smiles. . . .

CHAPTER FOUR: *The Black Mist*

KONARR rubbed his newly shaven chin as he watched the young thief enter the tavern tent after the lovely serving maid.

"A stupid job, this," he thought to himself, and muttered several choice curses. The musicians remained outside, and continued playing their wretched music.

Konarr's head ached with the wails of the black-skinned boy's skirlings, which he neither liked nor understood. He pressed his hand to his forehead for a moment, and cursed again to feel the grotesquely foppish cap he wore, drooping low over his forehead almost to his eyes, in the latest fashion for men of the Lady Tza's court.

Durrekal—it was hard after twenty years to call the man Zantain—had insisted on the disguise, pointing out that the young love to remember the faces behind the swords they have met. So there was nothing for it but to hack off his beard, don foolish hat and foppish clothing, wear narrow uncomfortable boots that broke his characteristic soldier's stride into an unfamiliar kind of awkward hobble.

It must have worked, Konarr realized by now, for Tassoran had not given sign of recognizing him, even though the shifting crowds had brought them almost face to face several times.

"He will not expect to see you, in the first place," Zantain had said. "And, dressed like a nincompoop of the court as you are, he will not give you a second glance even should his eye light on you."

"Nincompoop indeed," Konarr had muttered angrily, damning Zantain and himself for the humiliation he felt. "If any of my men were to see me like this, and recognized me, I

121

should have to fight each man in my entire Free Company before I should be permitted to lead them again!"

"Then it is fortunate you have revoked all leaves and passes during your absence on your own leave," said Zantain equitable. "You need not fear being recognized by anyone who knows you, not looking like that!"

Now it was getting late in the afternoon. Shadows were lengthening from the low towers of the Patricians' Quarter, west of the marketplace.

Hunger and thirst gnawed at Konarr's vitals. Being unskilled at tracking a man through city ways, he had not dared to take his eyes from Tassoran long enough to order a platter of food and to drink a stoup of ale.

But now he felt he understood the lad and his movements much better. It was reasonably certain that the fellow would stay in that tavern tent long enough for a starving soldier to wolf down a few bites of meat and gravy-soaked bread, and wet it down with rich brown ale.

He waited a moment to see that Tassoran would not immediately reemerge from the tavern.

Then he walked slowly past it, attempting to show as little overt interest as possible in the glimpse through the tent flap of a young man with his arms round a girl's waist, with the sound of laughter in two voices.

He sighed to himself, feeling a wave of inexplicable longing almost overwhelm him.

Then he walked on past the tavern to another nearby.

Tassoran laughed, half-intoxicated with the strong wine he had drunk, and the touch of the girl as he held her close.

But one quick kiss, and Iala darted away, laughter in her intense blue eyes.

"Nay, now," she said, "your money buys music, it buys drink, and even food. Thus your soul and body are tended to —do not think you can buy mine!"

He laughed again and shook his head. "It is too early in the day besides, fair miss," he said, chuckling.

A chunk of bread still stood on his platter, one forlorn piece amidst a small body of gravy. He seized the bread and vigorously attempted to sop up the entirety of the gravy with it, and very nearly managing.

Then he stood up.

"I have much to see to today," he announced, and allowed himself to be pleased to think the girl's face fell.

He placed a large worn silver queen down on the table beside the platter, lifted the small cup of wine and drained off what remained, and wiped his lips with the back of his hand. The coin was three times what the meal was worth, at the least. He felt a qualm, then reminded himself that he was a master thief with two peerless diamonds in his belt and a plan to steal a great and powerful magic artifact . . . he could afford it, and he would not soon return to Zetri after tomorrow night . . .

There was a whisper of canvas, and the ten-year-old drummer entered.

"Most generous master," he said, speaking quickly, "it is the custom of those of us who run free in the market place not to carry a tale to one who is not of us, unless we have been specifically hired. Let it then be said that by your generosity you have hired us! For we would not like to see you come to harm.

"For, noble sir, there are men who follow you through this marketplace!"

Tassoran frowned and started for the tent flap to look for himself.

"Nay, master," said the boy hastily, "do not look for them while standing in a doorway. Should you see one of them, he will surely realize it and you will never see him more—and we your loyal servants might not notice a later substitute . . ."

At that, Tassoran halted in his tracks, filled with sudden dismay and anger at himself.

"These last three days have reft me of my senses," he said bitterly aloud, not caring in his self-disgust who heard him.

Had he been as inept with the grown devlet that had been slavering after him, he would long since have been a fully digested meal . . .

"I am grateful to you, boy. There's more coins for you and your fellows, if you'll aid me further—as I seem to need help." The sarcasm in his voice was aimed at himself.

The boy nodded. "I am called Habu—Habu the Fleet. My brother who plays the horn is Chamon, and our friend who

123

plays the screaming skins of 'dzal is called Vallasz Venai. We are yours, noble sir."

"I am Tassoran, of . . ." He paused almost imperceptably, noting with satisfaction that Habu the Fleet had caught the hesitation in his voice. He decided to leave it at that. "Tell me the dress and manner of the pair that follow me, Habu, that I may be aware of my enemy."

"Enemies, noble sir," said Habu. "For from what we have observed, the two that follow you know not each other, nor have any interest in each other. One is dressed in the manner of the Lady's court, though he is ill-favored to be any sort of a true and gentle man for our mistress. The other, noble sir, wears grey . . ."

Among the common people, the poor, and the young, it was considered ill luck to speak too directly of any magick worker, and most especially if that one were a Spellmaster of Sezain.

Tassoran nodded. "Shagon does not trust me, it would seem," he thought to himself, pleased with himself for his calm.

"A short man, eh? The Sp—the one in grey, I mean. And a sheen of sweat lies on his face?"

Habu's forehead creased.

"Nay, master," he said, shaking his head. "The grey one is tall and slender, much like yourself in height. We cannot, of course, see his face for the cowl, save that Chamon says he saw the man's eyes, and they burned brightly. Which does not surprise me, considering," the lad said, with surprising calm.

"*Not* Shagon, then," Tassoran said aloud, and frowned himself. "I cannot understand . . ."

"Let them follow you, sir," Habu said eagerly. "We will resume our wanderings, but we shall stay near you. Presently we may know more about these strangers . . ."

Tassoran laughed and slapped his hands together. "We'll lead them a chase!" he said. "I meant to wander the market-place—well, now I'll make them walk till they wear out their boots! Why," he went on, caught up with the spirit, "how can they outlast me, who walked half across Senthar not three fifty-days since, and outdistanced a full-grown devlet! Court fops and piddling wizards, faught!"

Habu's urchin face split in a wide grin, exposing teeth already stained with chewing gwil-leaf; but he placed a finger to his lips. "They should perhaps not hear you be so gleeful, master," he cautioned, and Tassoran nodded.

"We go, then, fair Iala," Tassoran said to the serving girl, swatting at her behind affectionately and making her emit a startled gasp. "Habu, can you lead us back here when the day is done and the game's played out? My mistress's fair blue eyes have witched me, and I would return when duty—" and he chuckled, "—does not call!"

"Who does not know where the Inn of the Hangman lies?" said Habu, innocence bland on his sly face.

Tassoran blinked, and stared at the girl with the fiery blue eyes, trying to formulate a question.

"An ill omen, true," Iala said slowly. "Such a name is not of the normal sort. It is why Chousa has never had a signboard made. Yet," she added defiantly, "his many customers know he is one of the Lady's hangmen, and they understand."

Unsettled by the portent, Tassoran persisted. "But why do you work here? Are you his slave? I see no such markings on your fair skin, but—"

"Chousa is a friend of my late father, and our families owe each other . . . certain things. Thus from time to time I am found here, helping Chousa. The omen is ill but, I assure you, no one yet who has drunk Chousa's wine has found himself being served by Chousa elsewhere—and elsewise."

Tassoran thought that an overly cryptic way of referring to Chousa's profession as hangman, but Zetri people were not Kazemi, nor were their ways the same. He shrugged.

"I fear no omens," he said, smiling. "Especially when so beautiful a maiden assures me there's no harm . . . We shall return, Iala, before—"

He paused to think for a quick moment, considering the time of the year and the cycles of the moons.

"—before the three moons are all risen. As for now, we go!"

He clapped Habu on the shoulder, then strode vigorously out the tent flap into the crowded paths. There was no grey cowl in sight that he could see in one swift casual glance, but

125

within the flap of a nearby tent he thought he could make out a man in clothes of gaudy cut and color.

At that he smiled, but only to himself.

Konarr glanced up at the two moons speeding toward the zenith. Spea was in the lead, of course, with Fash lagging a good fifteen degrees. Instinctively Konarr looked to the north for Qul, and spotted her only a few degrees north of the horizon.

He nodded tiredly, too tired to bother to curse any more.

How long had it been, this day and night, since he had had time to cast himself down on a bench and rest even for five minutes? He could not say. He could only feel the protesting ache of muscles used as they had not been used in fifty fifty-days. Not even pursuing a band of marauders half across Tarmisorn compared with this day's labors!

Zantain would smile if he cursed the man, assuming Zantain was going to arrive for rendezvous—and Konarr touched his fingers to the hidden pouch wherein lay one of the two cold firewasps he had first seen three nights ago.

The firewasp was no longer chill in its small leather nest, but was distinctly warm to the touch. It was beginning to awaken, to realize its—mate, was the other? no one knew what the firewasps really were—fellow was absent.

Which meant that time was getting short, and that if Zantain did not arrive by midday tomorrow, the firewasp would take its own course of action . . .

He went back to wondering why he was supposed to be following Tassoran. Zantain had mentioned in passing that it was most important that nothing happened to Tassoran; that Konarr was, if necessary, to act to protect the lad.

Then he cursed, for it was Konarr who needed protection, against the younger man's tireless legs!

Konarr knew the marketplace, had visited it many times. Over twenty years he had covered much of it, following along all the twisting patchwork of tents and paths and wide-ways.

Today it was as if he had retraced every step he had taken in all those twenty years. How it was that a mere youth could so weary a trained, hardened, mercenary soldier, Konarr could not comprehend, except that walking was not the same

126

as marching, and that court boots were fit only to be burned.

When dusk came, he had even gone so far as to take a chance on losing Tassoran, by stopping to quickly purchase a worn but serviceable pair of guardsman's boots. They didn't match the colorful costume Zantain had forced on him, but Konarr dismissed this point with a curse for the man's black soul, and bought the boots anyway.

But the harm to his feet and legs had already been done, and hence, hours later, Konarr looked at Qul, slowly creeping upward from the horizon, and had not even the strength to summon up one more original obscene blasphemy.

There was a hiss and a bright flair of flames, as the fire in a nearby torch suddenly devoured a lump of pitch.

A motion near the flare caught his eye—a hooded figure, stepping hastily back between two tents.

Grey hood? The moons flooded the marketplace with their cold eerie light, washing out all normal colors and transforming the scene to a pastel revery.

Konarr could not tell if the hood had been truly grey, but in his mind there was no question about its having been a Spellmaster. This realization would have surprised him, had he not been weary past words to express.

The dim figure was gone now, and Konarr felt no urge to follow after it. His duty was still to Tassoran, it seemed—and it also seemed that Tassoran was safe for the night within the tavern to which he had recently returned.

Wild discordant music poured from the tent across the path, adding to Konarr's irritation. During the afternoon and evening he had been plagued with music, a constant stream of meaningless sound. Only the beat of the gnar-skin drum one half-weaned brat was thumping made any sense to him.

Konarr spat with disgust—and turned too late at the slight rustling sound behind him.

Iala was smiling her familiar lazy smile at Tassoran when the skinny form of Habu the Fleet darted in through the tent-flap, and the lad's urgent whisper broke Tassoran's sensuous concentration on the wench.

Scowling with irritation as he was, he could see her own brows knit with attention to the words . . .

"Master, the two who follow you—outside, now, the Spellmaster has taken the court buffoon, from behind, and questions him at knifepoint!"

And Habu stood there, abashed, realizing what kind of scene he had broken into.

Tassoran leaped up with a laugh. "Ha! They quarrel amongst themselves—I'll confront them both, and at my own advantage!"

Completely ignoring Iala now, Tassoran moved to a tied-down flap at the side of the tent away from where Habu indicated the inquisition was occurring. Deftly untying the knots holding the flap shut, he slipped outside, telling Habu in a whisper to retie it.

Then he moved through the darkness, among the backs of other tents, swinging silently around behind the position of the two men who were so interested in him . . . until at last he could see them ahead, backs to him.

Swiftly he moved up behind the grey-cowled figure and, before the astonished Spellmaster could react, stepped around to face the two from the side.

At the same time, Tassoran's unsheathed sword lashed out and tapped the Spellmaster's knifehand sharply, bringing out several tiny drops of blood.

The Spellmaster began muttering a hasty incantation, but found Tassoran's swordpoint at his throat.

"Another word of your foul blasphemies, and my sword goes through your neck, evil one!"

As Tassoran spoke, watching the Spellmaster's eyes drop in recognition of the situation, he realized the other man, the begauded dandy, was shifting his position, perhaps reaching for some perfumed weapon.

Perfumed or not, it would likely be dangerous, he realized, and began to wonder for the first time if he could control two men with just one sword.

Immediately he cursed himself for a wench-dazzled fool, and drew his throwing knife.

"Fellow," he said to the dandy, and then noticed his muscular build clearly for the first time. He paused for a moment to think about that, then decided that it made no difference.

He flourished the deadly little knife at the dandy. "Fellow, I could kill you with this at a distance of five tents, even in this gloom and half-light. So hold your peace, and do not move about quite so much. Especially do not move your hands, which I see are those of a swordsman though your clothes are those of a fop. I will speak with you in a moment. First I wish to address this sinister one."

Tassoran turned his attention back to the Spellmaster, whose eyes gleamed ferally out from under his cowl.

And Tassoran's eyes narrowed.

"Take the cowl from your head, Spellmaster," he said in a low tone, a new and dangerous edge in his voice.

The Spellmaster made as if to shake his head, then changed his mind.

Slowly he reached up, took the front of his cowl in his hands, and drew the cowl back off his head.

"*Taher!*" It was all Tassoran could say for the moment.

"Taher Kmatis now, my brother," said the Spellmaster. "Named and landed. Have you stolen as well as I have conjured, little thief?"

Tassoran swallowed with emotion, then bit back an angry reference to the gems concealed in his belt. Next he would be telling of tomorrow's venture!

"He is speechless, strange one," Taher Kmatis observed, turning toward the dandy, "as you were, even after I tried to persuade you with my dagger. Perhaps my brother would be interested in why this imbecile stranger masquerading as an intimate of the court has been following you about in your scramblings here and there today?"

Tassoran found his voice at last. "Oh, no. I am far more interested in you, dear brother. I know that you too have trod in my footsteps this long day through, quite as attentively as this . . . masquerader did.

"And I wonder why, dear brother. But more than that, I prefer that you would simply draw your sword, for that would solve all questions between us."

"Bah! You do not deserve the chance!" said Taher Kmatis, and flicked his left little finger at his younger brother.

A little spray of dust trailing after the finger toward the ground suddenly sprang outward in a black cloud, which quickly billowed further outward, then upward.

"You'll see again in a few minutes," laughed Taher Kmatis, as his voice faded into the distance.

Tassoran cursed among absolute darknesses, each one different from the last one a second ago, but each one totally impenetrable. Of course the other one would take the chance to leave too.

"You had no business asking foolish questions," Taher Kmatis' voice came, even further away. Tassoran attempted to stumble toward him, but could not hold a straight course to the sound.

"Ah, yes, young brother, you have missed a magic chance, indeed, this night—you should have killed me the moment you recognized me! Now you will suffer . . . and know you are doomed! If not tomorrow, then next fiftyday or next year, but when it happens it will happen, and you, oh brother, will die more hideously than you can now conceive . . ."

It was a last shout of defiant victory.

Tassoran cursed viciously and then cursed even louder as his shin collided with a splintered tent peg, knee high and more than sapling thick.

Then he laughed to himself, alone in the blackness, and sat down, with care, in the roadway.

After all, he reflected almost cheerfully, the blackness *would* lift, and he could make his way back to the Hangman's Inn, and Iala, and perhaps with her he could rest more contentedly than with Shagon of Shassa. He chuckled contentedly.

And then tomorrow eve and an exploit they'd write ballads on, from Tarmisorn to Kazemi!

He sat on the ground and drew a simple mandala of good cheer on the ground, and waited for the blackness to shred apart and leave the wholesome midnight, moons, clouds, and stars once more . . .

CHAPTER FIVE: *To the Charnel Pits!*

In IALA's sleeping tent, dizzy with strange strong brews and pipes, he awoke only once in the dream rich night, as small lives were beginning to move in the patches of grass outside the tents among man's artifacts, signaling ancient dawn and dawn's eternal ways.

There was movement among the sleeping robes, and warm spicy breath once more close to his face.

She whispered: "You said last night you did not need to rise till noon. I did not tell you I must leave much sooner. Goodbye, and live for a few more hours among the dream . . ."

And she was gone, and Tassoran drifted back into the full force and swell of the splendid raging epic that was the finest dream he yet had dreamt . . .

But after two hours, he awoke. His mind was clear, as she had told him it would. No muddle; good. Shagon would expect to see him by sun's zenith, and then there would be the afternoon and early evening for the final preparation.

It went along well, quite according to plan, for some time.

Late in the afternoon, after the final details had been worked out, Tassoran lay down once more on the low couch in Shagon's room, and the Spellmaster lit a torch that gave off a hideous stench.

Tassoran gagged once, then fell silent as Shagon himself lay down on another low couch.

Then the Spellmaster began a low incantation; it was repetitive, and Tassoran knew he was supposed to begin chanting along with Shagon as soon as he could pick up the words.

Presently they were both chanting in low tones.

Then things faded, and they were in the qen-trance that

prepared an adept—or one who had been prepared for temporary qen-trance—for supreme effort.

When the sun went down, they would awaken, and they would proceed to the outer walls of the Queen's Quarter, and after that, onward to the resting place of the Sigil of Tron itself . . .

Konarr's legs hurt that morning. With some effort he got his own boots on, after pitching the two he'd bought yesterday out the window. Then he checked the firewasp in its special pouch, for the first time that morning.

It was hot!—as hot as if fresh from the flame, and he yanked his hand from the pouch. Then quickly he untied the thong that held the pouch to his belt and placed the pouch on the table. He had no desire to stand near a firewasp when it chose to rouse itself and fly to its mate—burning its way through anything that chanced to be in its way!

But the heat also meant that the other firewasp might be getting nearer—this was, after all, the purpose in carrying them: to rendezvous.

Konarr was taking no chances, just because he had been told the wasp would not fly till noon.

There came a commanding knock at the door, and Zantain entered, looking taller and more vigorous than the last time they had met.

Immediately upon entering, he saw the pouch on the table, went to it, and placed it next to a similar pouch on his own belt.

There was silence for a moment.

"There, they should have gotten over it by now," said Zantain, and, plucking Konarr's firewasp out of its pouch, he placed it inside the other pouch.

For one more timeless moment Konarr felt a wave of thankful, joyous relief flow over him, the emotional backwash sweeping out from the rejoining of the firewasps.

When it was done he sat down immediately, blinking his eyes and trying to catch his breath.

Zantain sat with even more evident relief, which did not surprise Konarr, since the firewasps were his and hence more in tune with him.

Presently they had regained sufficient composure after the

backwash to talk, and Zantain wanted simply to know what had occurred.

It went with no comment till Konarr broke off to ask about the Spellmaster who had waylaid him.

Zantain waved the Spellmaster aside. "If he is our Tassoran's elder brother, what is between them is irrelevant to our course unless the brother returns to interfere before we're done. His last words sound as if he were disgusted at having been detected, and was prepared to go off for some while to prepare some new attack. It is also possible he came nosing after the treasure in Shagon's footsteps, and hoped his brother might unwittingly provide some key.

"What interests me is this Iala. They crept off, those two, did they, while you were trying to find your way back to the inn after going the wrong way through the black mist. They could be anywhere. Have you checked this morning in Shagon's room with the device I left you?"

Konarr admitted he had just risen, being exceedingly tired by the previous day's exertions.

Zantain closed his eyes for a moment, opening them immediately. "They're both near here, and together."

"How did you find that out?" asked Konarr, wondering with jaw gaping.

"Teshel'direw mind-sweep," Zantain said. Then he blinked. "Forget I said that." And Konarr blinked.

"How did you find that out?" asked Konarr, wondering with jaw gaping.

Zantain smiled. "Just testing you," he said. "I suspected you were too tired to have gotten up long before I arrived, from what you said, and—"

"No, no," Konarr said, and Zantain creased his brow in a small frown. "What made you think they are both here? I suspected he wouldn't be back until mid-afternoon, and—"

Zantain broke in with a smile. "I saw the lad before I reached the inn. The other one I knew was here—he gives off a smell of misused power."

Konarr dropped the matter, to Zantain's relief, and they worked out the final details of their plan.

"Secrets," thought Zantain. "I must be tired indeed if I'm giving them away . . ."

133

There was no reason for things to be quiet, Tassoran knew that; and thieves ofttimes work best in the midst of high festivity.

Nonetheless it seemed to him some special fever of gaiety infected the Lesser Palace, as he stole unseen through its halls. A wild profusion of musical instruments from all the New Lands played separate concerts in the intricately interacting architectural whimseys of the Lesser Palace. A screeing of harsh northland bagwinds cut across the ceremonious, solemn honking of priesthorns.

As this came just when Tassoran was tiptoeing uneasily past a Hawk Guard posted at the intersection of five corridors, he jumped involuntarily. Luckily he made no noise, so the guard paid no notice.

The Spellmaster, Tassoran considered, had done his job well no matter what his faults. With his deep magic spell, constantly muttered, Tassoran was a match for whomever he might meet—for they could not see him.

It was only a matter of sense of direction, to make his way through the labyrinthean corridors of the Lesser Palace to the inner walls, bordering on the garden at whose center rose the baleful Ebon Tower. And once through the Lesser Palace, there was but a simple walkway to the Ebon Tower, entering which would be simplicity since it had no doors, but only great soaring archways to its spacious interior.

Regretful that he could not put his newfound talent to some more entertaining use, such as slipping into one of the kitchens and toying with the scullery maids there—or with the Lady's own maids of waiting in the ballrooms—Tassoran made his way through the byway corridors.

He rounded a corner, and stopped, puzzled.

A short corridor led to a large room. There were no other corridors intercepting . . . a dead end. Now he'd have to retrace his steps past two Hawk Guards before getting back on to the other route. He cursed his carelessness, then turned to retrace his footsteps back to a more fortunate turning.

Iala stood there, dressed only in a thin transparent gown of rarest silk.

A thief's nerves must be strong, to bear up under the thousand strains that assail a man who is going about unsanctioned business in another man's dwelling. The mark of a

134

master thief is that nothing can disarm him of his calm while he is going about his work.

Tassoran instinctively began whispering the chant of invisibility louder, not even pausing to wonder why Iala was there at all. There was no time for questions and answers, not even for one. The timing had been carefully worked out, and did not allow for more than three wrong turnings as he made his way through the Lesser Palace.

Hence he was down to the thin edge of minutes before he must be outside again and making for the Ebon Tower itself, in the center of the inner courtyard bounded on this side by the Lesser Palace.

"Be quiet," said Iala, and clapped her hands.

Tassoran found his mouth frozen in a half-open position, in the middle of uttering the spell.

"Guards, ho," she called then, in a clear strong voice that penetrated the echoing corridors and the distant shouts of music and wild laughter.

From either end of the short corridor in which Iala and Tassoran stood, came squads of soldiers, all wearing the hawk head helmets.

The helmets of most of the soldiers were of bronze, glinting dully in the torchlight from the braziers in the age-blackened stone walls. Two helmets were silver, one for each squad, and one was inlaid with gold and bore an ivory disk with a mystic symbol inscribed upon it.

"High Captain Drammath," said the man with the gold-inlaid helmet. "My Lady Tza, this man made his way undetected past two dozens of my best men. How, I cannot understand, but—"

"Nor can I understand how this man came across the ancient spell of selective blindness," said Iala/Tza, while Tassoran, finding his jaw starting to work again, looked at her still thunderstruck. Even his iron nerves were shaken, to find the tavern wench of last night was really the eighth Lady Tza, absolute ruler of a land which extended over more territory than any other kingdom in the New Lands save for the vast central steppes of Senthar.

The Lady Tza, eighth of that name; who ruled all the land of Tarmisorn from the Queen City of Zetri; mistress of magic; enchantress of the winds and rains; so powerful a con-

jurer by reputation and in fact that only the mysterious Azeltarem, the utterly feared Black Magician himself, hidden in
his castle-palace in the gloom and shadow of Shaiphar Mountain, was said to be her equal . . .

Not for two thousand years, save once, had any challenged
the power of the line of ensorcelling queens, and so the many
lands to the east of Tarmisorn had known a kind of peace, as
did Tarmisorn itself. Nonetheless, the Lady Tza was ever
known to be a cruel monarch of her people, who did not hes-
itate to visit the most hideous magical vengeances upon those
who crossed her . . .

Tassoran pondered for a moment, now that he could almost move his jaws again and speak, whether he should attempt to use either of Shagon's other two magic devices.

But when he tried to flex his leg muscles, he found that he
could not move them at all.

"No," said Iala/Tza, the serving wench who ruled an age
old land, "you cannot move until I release you—which presently I shall. I keep you thus for now, that you may more
fully realize how hopeless is the position in which you have
put yourself. This enhances certain events that will come
upon you, but that is a bit later . . . Captain Drammath,"
she said, abruptly turning away from Tassoran, "have your
men take this one into my audience chamber and place him
at the central binding-post in front of my throne. I shall
move about the palace for a time to ascertain whether there
may be others like this one about, though I think there is not.
Then I shall return to pass my preliminary judgment upon
this man."

Tassoran felt himself seized on either side by guardsmen,
turned around, and carried toward the large chamber he had
earlier recognized as *not* where he wished to go. *So much for
my wishes,* he thought ruefully.

Then his back was placed against a black marble post almost as tall as he, and a band of pure yellow fire sprang into
existence around his waist.

Simultaneously with the appearance of the flame, he found
he could move again; his legs gave way with the sudden
shock and the flame touched his chest.

But the flame did not sear his flesh; instead, a lance of
total agony shot through his body. His legs stiffened straight

again instinctively, and the pain was gone the moment contact with the magic flame was broken. Tassoran sobbed for breath.

One of the silver-helmeted men protested to High Captain Drammath. "We know he can work in the mysteries," he said. "We should not allow the Lady to face any kind of danger, and those who work with spells can often cast them with hands and fingers, so that we would not even hear him speak."

Drammath thought a moment, then shook his head. "He is but a thief, the Lady told us. He has some small command of memorized incantations, but he is no master, nor even an apprentice, in the high arts. And ordinary spells will not work within the enchanted fire, at any rate. No, we shall not worry. It emphasizes his helplessness, which pleases the Lady . . ."

There was the sound of many footsteps in the audience chamber, behind and beyond the pillar to which Tassoran was chained by the yellow flames.

He writhed around the black marble pillar slowly and carefully, avoiding contact with the fire, until he was able to see part of what was occurring behind him.

Silent masses of people in every gaudy color and style were crowding in the main door of the chamber.

Uttering hardly a sound, but otherwise jostling and hurrying their way inside like any other group of curious folk, the court of the Lady Tza assembled.

He stared at them in astonishment as they viewed him in silent disdain. Ordinarily a taken thief was summarily beaten to death by whomsoever happened to take an interest in such matters—thrown to the crowd. At the least, there were insults and catcalls and boos and lumps of dung thrown at one.

The silence was unnerving.

Presently there was a light footstep in front of Tassoran, and he turned back to face the throne.

The Lady Tza stood there in her diaphanous gown.

Tassoran's mind whirled around the aspects of his situation, desperately seeking a way out when none appeared likely. But it was hard to concentrate; he had had several nasty surprises in the last few minutes.

And there was the Lady Tza, her beauty, her commanding

137

presence—and the nakedness of her fair body under the gown. He shut his eyes reflexively for a moment, wondering whether he had actually slept with this incredible woman . . . and found his memory would not tell him. He had had his arms about her, this he knew; and he had kissed those lips, warm and soft then, harsh and cruel now.

The Lady Tza sat down slowly on her ivory throne, traced with gold and silver designs of fearful beasts and studded with delicately varied gems and stones.

"I will keep you alive for ten fiftydays," said the Lady Tza addressing Tassoran directly and without preamble. "You will be intricately tortured during that period, of course."

There was a murmur at last from the mass of courtiers. Approval? wondered Tassoran. Or were they as revolted as decent folk would be? The way to dispose of a thief was to tear him apart immediately, not torture him!

"These," said the Lady Tza, gesturing languidly at the assembled courtiers, "are my creatures, oh thief who would do great deeds. It matters not what I tell them or say about them, though I do not tell them everything.

"They do not care that you will be tortured, although they will delight to observe those sessions at which I will permit them to be present.

"They also do not care why you were caught, but I will tell you something of that, for it will tell you even more about the hopelessness of your position."

The Lady Tza arose from her ivory throne and walked slowly, delicatedly, toward the fire-chained thief, her perfect breasts quite visible through her thin robe and the rest of her body no mystery, though Tassoran did not dare to look. He was careful to look only at her eyes, pale blue eyes with a fiery eagerness behind them.

She paused, standing almost against the circlet of flames.

"I foresaw some interference with my desire to hold the Sigil of Tron, to master its depths and mysteries, and to use it to conquer all the New Lands."

Tassoran caught his breath at this casual revelation, as she continued.

"Iala is but one of my disguises; my lore told me that if I spent some days at the Inn of the Hangman, I would learn more of who threatens the sigil.

"You came. And now you are here.

"And in ten fiftydays, you will meet Chousa—no, you drank his wine. You shall instead meet Chava, his brother. And you will die."

"Well," said Tassoran, shifting his legs slightly to ease the cramp from standing rigidly away from the belt of magic flames, "if this chamber is to be my home for ten fiftydays, I suppose I should begin to acquire a taste for it . . ."

The Lady Tza smiled. "It will be amusing to see just how long you retain that sense of humor you are so proud of! But do not think this audience chamber is for the likes of you to scream in, thief. You are not so handsome nor so important."

She leaned across the flame till her breasts touched his chest, for a moment. "It will be even more interesting to see how long it takes for your dreams to fade," she said, and her tone was now more langorous than ever. "It is my special fancy to add myself, as it were, into the delightful equations of your physical and mental agonies. Your former dream of me was false.

"And that is the last true thing that you will ever know for certain, save for pain."

She stepped back from him, and clapped her hands.

A small pie-shaped split appeared in the circle of flooring at the foot of the pillar to which Tassoran was chained.

With a jerk, the split widened rapidly until Tassoran had no footing left and began to fall. The flame disappeared then, as he dropped, and he made one desperate lunge with his arms to catch the solid edge of the chamber floor.

One hand caught for a moment, but warm, strong, feminine fingers swiftly and easily dislodged it.

He fell into blackness.

CHAPTER SIX: *The Vapor of Death*

STUNNED MOMENTARILY by his fall, Tassoran blinked and waited, hoping some chink of light would reveal his situation beyond the fact that he was in a barred cell. The floor above had closed by the time he had thudded heavily into the stone floor of what, from the charnel stench and incredible foetor, might well be a wild animal pit.

He ran through other possibilities, discarding dangerous animals on the loose here since it was unlikely the Lady Tza would place him where he would die unseen.

Hunger? Much more likely—perhaps as part of the torture itself. But that would not be a problem immediately.

Other prisoners?

Guards?

There was only one way to tell, and he hallooed as loudly as he could manage, not having gotten all his breath back from the fall, though he had landed catlike and uninjured. No answer came.

But was he uninjured? As he lay on the chill stone, he wondered; then he tried to get up, and instantly felt pain in one ankle. Testing it, he decided it wasn't broken, and shouted again.

His voice echoed strangely in the unknown depths of the barred pit chamber, and died away.

Tassoran shuddered in spite of himself. He didn't mind loneliness, he told himself. It was just that he liked to pick his own time to be alone . . .

. . . He could not tell how much time had passed before he finally heard some distant noise reverberating through the pit. It took a moment for him to sort it out through the blurring echoes.

It was the sound of a metal lock being opened. The creak

of the door as it opened was hidden by distance, but a moment later came a much louder sound. Tassoran had no difficulty in identifying it as a heavy metal door clanging shut.

Quietly rising to his feet, he had limped away from the place he had landed—how long before?—and came presently to a stone wall, wet and lichenous to his touch.

There he waited.

Presently there was the sound of footsteps. At least two men, he thought first; then he amended his count to two only.

The footsteps became clearer, closer. Uncertain as to what he should—or could—do, especially in the endless blackness, he stood silently waiting.

Then there was a glimmer of torchlight, round a distant corner.

It seared his eyes and he turned away after the first gleam, hoping he would have time to adjust his eyesight before . . . before what? He sighed aloud then, realizing there was nothing he could do beforehand.

A voice came, blurred with echo. "I want the very spot, you understand. No tricks. You must do it, by the power of the Tarnflower. And you had best hope he was not hurt in the fall."

Was there a familiar note in that voice?

Tassoran's eyes were becoming accustomed once more to light as the approaching torches cast wavering manic shapes of light and shadow on the bare wet stones of the caverns underneath the Lesser Palace.

Presently two figures appeared, down a stone-walled corridor—a helmetless guard, and someone in courtier's garb . . .

The courtier looked familiar—doubly familiar, in fact, because the torchs' flickering momentarily gave him the look of having a beard.

Konarr! The good captain of the Bephan garrison!

"Ho," said Tassoran, conversationally, as the two figures neared his cell, "good master Konarr, I am beholden for the sight of you. Though you have cropped your beard away and disfigured yourself with courtly style so much that I could not recognize you yesterday, it is good to see even so sad a figure, here in my condition . . ."

Konarr started at his opening words, almost dropping the torch and the drawn sword he carried. The guard with him stopped when he did and simply stood, arms at his side, as if waiting dumbly for more instructions—which Konarr immediately assured Tassoran was the case.

"It's a strange situation, and a strange story, lad," said Konarr, urgency in his voice, "and if you'll only let me tell you the all of it some *other* time, I will be much beholden to you and we can get along with the business of rescuing you. Then we can see to the stealing of the Sigil of Tron and escaping from this accursed city. And when I do explain it to you," he ended with a grimace, "you may entertain yourself attempting to invent a sensible explanation for why I ever went along . . ."

Tassoran found the strength to chuckle, and realized he was weak. "How long has it been since I entered the palace —as you are here, I presume you know that as well?"

"You entered at the stroke of the fourth hour of darkness. It is now the eighth hour."

Tassoran laughed. "All in all, I daresay you haven't said as much all together since the last time you called the muster of your Free Company, good captain! Almost you convince me . . ."

"Mmm," said the good captain. "Let me convince you by telling you you've no other choice. And I will admit to any man after tonight that this man Zantain sews a tight stitch for a man who's never been to sea . . ."

And Konarr drew the guardsman's sword and handed it through the bars to Tassoran, who examined it a moment, then sheathed it in his own empty scabbard. Then Konarr ordered the stupefied guard to unlock Tassoran's cell, then to lie down and go to sleep.

Then the two men started trudging through the pit corridors, each holding a torch high.

Tassoran harked back. "I did not know you were a man who'd gone beyond sight of land, Captain."

"What do you think I'd been doing the ten years before I . . . chose . . . to beach myself among a Free Company? Half around the New Lands I'd sailed, young thief, before I'd turned fifteen, and before I was sixteen I saw the rocky shoals that mark the olden coasts of Pazatar and Armassic themselves . . ."

Then Konarr fell silent, and Tassoran did not press him.

142

After some minutes of walking, Tassoran looked about to see that they were in a large chamber—and the only exit was the one they'd just come through. The floor was covered with rotting, indescribable muck.

"Where *are* we, and where are we going?" he whispered, speaking low instinctively.

"I have no idea what our path is," Konarr replied truthfully. "But Zantain told me I would find the way, and I am finding the way. I believe that he is actually guiding me, though physically I know he is now nowhere near the Queen's quarter. Such is magic, and I can't say I like it."

And he walked straight for the stone-walled rear corner of the room.

Tassoran's eyes narrowed and he could feel his heart slam wildly in his chest a moment.

For when Konarr reached the stone wall, the large slab that had been facing him was no longer there.

Before them, through the solid walls of the chamber, led a narrow, twisting, man-wide corridor!

Tassoran decided there was no sensible question to be asked about any of it all, followed the captain and said nothing.

It was like walking through odorless thin smoke.

"This palace," Konarr said, unusually talkative, "Zantain says, is a thousand and more years old, and he was one of the architects—he is a Longlived One, though he says he is not of their blood. The Lesser Palace was constructed with a maze of secret passages both above and below the ground, which the then Lady Tza, third of that name, delighted in using.

"Then there was a second set of passages, more skeletal in their network than the first, and known only to the Lady and to Vesalye the Wise—as Zantain called himself then. The dozen picked workmen who had constructed the doubly secret passages were carefully poisoned after, by the Lady, leaving only her and Zantain knowing a secret hidden even from her deepest, most solemn-trusted counsellors.

"She thought then to have Vesalye slain, to narrow the secret down to one. But he disappeared, and she never knew that Zantain had constructed a third set of secret passages. Now the Lady at first suspected this might have happened,

143

and from time to time did test this wall and that wall and the other in secret; but she found nothing.

"Zantain did not tell me all, but I know that the secret of these passages is a mystery of the mind rather than of locality, and hence we travel through the stone itself, though it seems we walk in a passageway . . ."

Tassoran gulped. "Through . . . the stone . . . itself?"

It was too much. Tassoran felt chilled to the inner fastnesses of his being with a sensation of stark terror that transfixed him at last where he stood.

"I . . . I can go no further," whispered Tassoran.

"He said we might feel thus," Konarr answered gruffly, and with the air of friendly persuasion, grasped Tassoran by the back of his neck and moved his hand inexorably forward.

Tassoran had to walk forward or be pitched headfirst to the . . . floor, was it? his mind gibbered for a moment . . .

He stepped forward stiffly, hardly able to realize he could move after that bolt of paralyzing fear.

"Forces . . ." he whispered, "such forces . . ."

Konarr muttered something indistinct, not meant to carry objective meaning and not taken so.

Tassoran gathered his thoughts a moment, as they resumed walking through the narrow corridor.

"What has he done for you?" he said then, in a rush. "You speak familiarly of things you cannot know, and travel a path—"

"He loaned me some skills," Konarr said, "just as the sweating Spellmaster loaned others to you. If we are fortunate, we may successfully combine our skills, oh valiant thief, and our wizards' tricks." He spat. "If you are a man with my nature," he said after a pause, "you would sooner be choosing your own path and your own weapons, eh?"

And he grinned.

At that, Tassoran's spirits returned, and his answer was a hearty laugh of assent. "But," he continued, "we must make the best of whatever we have, for the little that may be worth. I have lost some faith, I may tell you, in my squat Spellmaster—since I was chained with magic fire and cast into a slaughter pit. And, by the staff, I had performed all the rites correctly—he had bound me with other spells to do no

144

otherwise! Ha. Will I do no better with my remaining tricks?"

They came to a narrow winding descent of stairs.

"Untrodden by any not directed here by Zantain," Konarr said. "And how I know it, I cannot say."

"I do not think I care for these magics from nowhere that do so much for no reason I can see . . ."

"Zantain told me we would pay for what we do this night, in weeks to come. The magic uses our own strength. Which," Konarr said with sudden satisfaction, "is the real reason why all true men, like ourselves, commonly abhor magic."

They made their way down the narrow stairs, Konarr shifting slightly sidewise because his shoulders were too broad; they scraped the sides of the descending tunnel.

Tassoran cursed as he hit his head, when a sharp turn debouched onto a landing. The roof of the tunnel was now so much lower that even Konarr had to duck his head to continue.

They reached another landing.

There were no more stairs, either down or up.

There was no more tunnel.

There was only what amounted to a tiny room, big enough for two men to stand in, uncomfortably.

Tassoran rubbed his smooth jaw and found himself oddly contemplating the question of whether he was ever going to get a beard started.

Then he shook his head and looked about, seeing nothing. Already the smoke was collecting, and he stubbed out his torch, leaving only Konarr's.

"I . . . I do not understand," Konarr whispered. "I cannot tell what to do next. It is as if some . . . some sort of contact I had with . . . with Zantain's knowledge, had been dampened off by all this stone . . . but it's strange that I should think that, too . . ."

Tassoran covered his eyes with his hands for a moment, trying to collect thoughts that might help. Then he stared at the ceiling, hoping obscurely for helpful words there.

"Look there," he said urgently, after a brief time trying to sort out what he was seeing. "Isn't that a rung, up in the corner there? What's a rung doing at eye level in a closed room with no other exit but the way we came?"

145

"Bake in hell fire," said Konarr, "and I would tell you nothing, for I cannot. Perhaps . . . perhaps I took a wrong turning back there somewhere. Let us return some way along our path, retrace our footsteps . . . we may discover a better path."

"Ha!" said Tassoran. "You spoke before of a mystery of the mind. Perhaps we do not have your quiet little voice guiding you, for the moment, but we still have our minds. Suppose, then, that that rung were the first of a series of rungs, running upward so to the surface, and suppose we were directly below the Ebon Tower . . ."

"But the roof is solid stone!"

"You should ponder the mysteries you walk with more thoroughly, my friend," said Tassoran, vastly pleased with himself. "We have walked through stone tonight before, have we not? We have only to do so now, and by the time we near the surface, why, either your magician will aid you once more, or mine will. I have, after all, two more surprises . . ."

Konarr shrugged. "Perhaps—but you may lead!"

At that Tassoran frowned, but immediately laughed. "Of course! So then, let us be off!"

"Yes, indeed," Konarr said, but waited for Tassoran to move. After the lad had cracked his head on the stone ceiling, they could retrace their steps and—

Tassoran grasped the lone rung firmly, then straightened up so that his head touched the ceiling . . .

. . . and as his head touched the stone, his head continued to move upward as he began to climb.

For the stone ceiling had vanished: above them was a narrow, perpendicular shaft, rungs laddering upward . . .

After proceeding upward half a dozen rungs, Tassoran looked down at Konarr, still standing on the floor of what had seemed a tiny room—and which now seemed only the bottom of a smoky, immensely deep well—and Tassoran laughed.

"Come on, old captain!" he called down, "we have a great deal of climbing indeed, and we should not disappoint our magicians!"

"So! We are within the walls of the Ebon Tower itself," whispered Tassoran.

Reaching the top of the shaft at last, he had climbed out silently to look about for guards, while Konarr remained several rungs down, out of sight. Though they were not magicians, they could feel the auras of power that centered on the Ebon Tower, and were determined to take no chances.

Tassoran found himself in a small room, with curving corridors leading from it in opposite directions. It took only a moment for him to establish that this was another of Zantain's smoky tunnels in the stone, and that this time the stone was that of the Tower itself.

There were even occasional peepholes—both inward, to the chambers of the Tower, and outward, overlooking the gardens that surrounded the massive stone edifice.

He helped Konarr over the edge of the pit then, and Konarr complained that it had been like climbing a thousand stories. Tassoran himself was soaked with sweat, but was also determined not to complain.

Besides, it was not time for him to get down to business—*his* business, *his* specialty—and secretly he was delighted to have the chance at last to try out the other tricks Shagon had loaned him.

Silently, carefully, they made their way through the narrow corridor running through the walls themselves, checking through the peepholes to be sure of missing nothing of possible significance.

"Ho!" whispered Konarr suddenly. "There it is again!"

"What?"

"My . . . my knowledge. It's back. Come on, we have to do some more climbing. Back to the room the pit opened onto!"

Set in the inner wall of the small room were more rungs, running both upward and downward. Tassoran sighed, and allowed Konarr to lead the way upward.

After two levels Konarr stopped climbing and got off the rungs, in another small room. He checked the nearest inner peephole.

There was a long pause.

Finally, Konarr stepped back into the wall. "Look," he said, indicating the peephole. "How do you propose to solve that problem?"

Tassoran looked through the peephole.

There was a large stone-walled chamber, plain, unoccupied —save for strangely solid-looking wisps of orange vapor that hung about the room, being wafted gently about by some mysterious breeze.

Or so it appeared.

"I don't know what that vapor in there is," said Tassoran, "and why should it concern us, at any rate?"

"That is where the sigil is," Konarr said. "Please spare me questions as to how I know. It is simply *there*, and you, my thief, must find a way . . ."

"How is it that we walk within half a dozen steps of her innermost secret tresures of magic, and she knows nothing? Surely your Zantain can—"

Konarr shook his head slowly. "No, he cannot solve our problem," he said inexorably. "You must find and steal the Sigil of Tron, and we must escape from this place. How? Now the problems are yours—even finding the sigil would be beyond me."

"Do not worry about me finding the sigil. I am a thief; I have studied the arts of concealment. I am worrying about that vapor, for I cannot be sure what it is and what it implies —and what it may do to me when I enter that chamber. So. Your friend tells you no more? I could use counsel . . ."

"No," Konarr said again, slowly, and looked through the peephole again. "I have nothing for you from him except about the passages through stone. And except that I think that vapor may be no ordinary vapor at all, friend Tassoran. Look you, it does not dissipate, nor do I spy any place in that room from whence the vapor has come."

Tassoran nodded.

"I think," Konarr continued, "that I would not like to enter that room, for I think that orange vapor may be from the crushed flowers of the gravedust plant, which is death."

"A message at last," said Tassoran, grinning in spite of himself. "Now how do I stay alive?"

"Use Shagon's tricks."

"One was a spell of invisibility, of no use here—and I cannot use it again at any rate. Another is a phrase I may whisper to strike any man loose from his memories. But I prefer my sword, and there are no men in the room anyway. And the third grants me some handsful of minutes when, Shagon

148

told me, no man in this land could catch me, so fast would I be able to run. He warned me to touch no one while working this incantation, for it would affect him the same way. At least when we leave, we will then be able to leave together."

"Unpromising," Konarr admitted grudgingly. "And the gravedust fumes are attracted to life, so that if you come near them, they come nearer and nearer to you, though they cannot move with great speed . . ."

Konarr stopped and looked at Tassoran, who thought a moment, then cocked his head and slowly nodded, seeing a plan unfold. "That leaves the question of how to get into that room, and how to get out of this tower."

"We are three floors above the paving outside," Konarr said. "Then there is the moat, which legend—and loose-tongued Hawk Guards from the Queen's Quarters—says hold gaphalon and kannaq and virionne, and only the Lady Tza can pass safely over the waters at one slender footbridge. . ."

Tassoran sighed deeply. "I should have refused this commission. That much is clear. What if we were to descend once more into the pit, and thence from the bottom retrace our steps through the caverns underneath the Lesser Palace? We could then leave by the same method which gained you entrance, and safely we could be away from this place."

Konarr shook his head. "Five guards died near the spot where I entered the Queens' Quarter, and three more at the spot where I found the first underground passage leading to your sector of the pits. I do not think that way will be clear again until we have been slain—or leave in some other fashion. For that, I think, you will need all your conjurer's speed."

It was Tassoran's turn to shake his head. "We are peering too far into the future. There is the matter of a problem here, and now—the fumes, probably deadly, and the Sigil of Tron, which does not seem to be within the room."

"As for the sigil," Konarr answered, "you have spoken it —you are the professional thief, not I. As for the fumes . . . Zantain should have come himself. I can get you into this room, but I cannot do more."

"There are only two possibilities," Tassoran mused, "one being that the sigil is hidden within the stone walls of the chamber, and the other . . ."

While Tassoran fell silent and worked on his problem, Konarr paced restlessly along the narrow tunnel, galled to be turned so completely useless in a moment, simply because he was neither a magician nor a thief.

He watched Tassoran study the interior of the chamber as well as he could through the limits of the peephole. A soldier was of no use in such complex affairs, even though it made his blood tingle and run faster through his veins, made him hate the thought of returning to garrison duty on the Oulan Road, sameness unending for fifty fiftydays . . .

Konarr grunted with anger and peered through the next outside peephole. Deep within him an uneasyness was growing.

He was looking to the west from three stories up in the Ebon Tower. Looming largest was the fiery blaze of the Lesser Palace, whether candlelight or witchfire Konarr could not tell. Plainly, though, the Lady was unnerved, supposed some malign influence to be working in the Lesser Palace, was taking precautions . . . and was looking in the wrong place!

At that Konarr grinned, though the double ring of guards round the Lesser Palace had its own ominous overtones.

Of course, the two of them had not intended returning through the Lesser Palace, but so many men, all wearing the Hawk Helmets, even as he did—for a moment the thought of lifting sword against what in a sense were his own men made him frown, trying to work it out. Of course, he had already slain eight . . .

He decided that answers would be meaningless if they did not escape, and Zantain had made it plain what would happen if that happened. So there was only the present question, and a glance at Tassoran showed he did not seem close to answering it.

Konarr moved to the inner peephole, facing the guardroom. It was almost a pleasure to see only two guards, instead of two thousand.

But they weren't really *guards*, Konarr realized after a moment. They wore the scarlet short-cloak of the Queen's Personal Guard, but they were dressed in casual fashions of the court apart from that.

Konarr looked about the room for a moment, then saw

150

two cuirasses sitting on the floor, side by side—ready for use should someone dare to question whether young nobility were properly performing its duty.

Obviously it was considered more an honorary position than a practical or necessary one, at least by the two nobles, which fit what he had gleaned of court ways in the last twenty years.

On a nearby table in the guardroom stood three goblets, two of richly chased silver, one of plain unstained wood, dark and cracked with age.

As Konarr watched, one of the nobles reached for a silver cup and drained it, then refilled the cup from a gallon flask of leather bound with straps of silvery thread.

Konarr shrugged and continued around the walls of the Ebon Tower, checking each outer and inner peephole until after some minutes he came once more on Tassoran.

Tassoran was sitting on the floor, his legs crossed.

"Are you thinking, or simply clearing your mind for death?" Konarr said, chuckling. "You look as relaxed as those lazy fops in the next chamber, pretending they're guards—drunken louts! If they spent a fiftyday in *my* Free Company . . . well, I wish Zantain had a tunnel into *that* chamber."

"What?" said Tassoran, blinking as he tried to remember what Konarr had said.

"Why, if I could make my way into the guardroom, we could kill the two guards, and . . . and . . ." He floundered for a moment.

Tassoran gave Konarr a sour look. "And then stand there and wonder how to get into the inner chamber from *that* side, eh? Killing a couple of guards hardly solves the problem of the poisonous fumes."

Konarr frowned. "How do the *guards* get inside, then?" he asked. "They may not be soldiers, but still they must go by a routine, and therefore there must be some way for them to enter the inner chamber. Doesn't that seem reasonable?"

"Why?" asked Tassoran. "Only the Lady should need to enter the chamber. I should think she would not want even her nobility to know what lies within—she said as much to me, or so I understood her. No doubt, as Shagon intimated to

151

me, she wipes their minds free after they leave. She would take no chances."

"Bah," Konarr said. "Of course she would take chances. Why should she be uneasy in the heart of her kingdom, on her own palace grounds, in the Ebon Tower. She and her predecessors have held power for so long that—"

"Tell me what you saw in the next room again," said Tassoran, struck by a sudden thought. "Quickly. I have an idea."

Irritated at the interruption, Konarr grumbled. But he described the guard chamber once more.

"*Three* cups," said Tassoran softly. "Then there can be no doubt of it—she worked a transformation, and a mightily powerful one. Look you, that orange vapor is instant death —how is *she* to enter? No, I am sure the guards have means whereby they can avoid the fumes. Unquestionably."

"What do you mean?" Konarr demanded, angered at this mystification.

"Never mind. Just use your Zantain's handy knack—open the way inside this chamber filled with death."

"But the vapor will enter the corridor here—we will die!"

"Do it," Tassoran said.

And he laughed.

CHAPTER SEVEN: *The Sigil of Tron*

KONARR creased his forehead. "There will be one stone that must be moved physically," he said slowly. "We can move through the wall at . . . *this* point," he continued, moving his hands along the wall as he spoke and stopping finally at a lighter-colored slab. "The slab on the inner wall of the chamber is solid but not thick, and it pivots."

He stepped forward into the stone wall, stooping a bit, and the stone vanished, leaving a small dead end tunnel. Then he reappeared. "This is your part of the game," he said ."After you . . ."

Tassoran entered the small tunnel and pressed his shoulder against the inner slab.

For a moment nothing happened. Tassoran increased the pressure, and the slab shifted a trifle.

Slightly more pressure . . . and the slab pivoted silently open.

Hastily Tassoran drew back from the opening and observed the fumes in the chamber, as they wafted slowly toward him. He crouched in the tunnel, ready to propel himself backward to safety if the fumes moved past the boundary of their chamber.

But they did not, hovering instead in a thin orange haze around the pivoted slab.

"Now what?" asked Konarr.

"Check at the guardroom peephole," Tassoran said after a moment's consideration. "I'm going to cause a stir and I want to know what the guards do before they actually get in here —or raise an alarm."

"Mmmm," said Konarr. "Right. I suppose we must take the chance."

Konarr went to the guardroom peephole.

Tassoran drew the sword Konarr had taken from the Hawk Guard that had been left sleeping in the charnel pits.

Then, holding the blade with the aid of a piece of cloth, he stuck the pommel through the opening into the chamber and began banging it noisily against the floor.

The vapors shifted slightly, but menaced him no more than before.

"That fetched them," Konarr called, as once more Tassoran withdrew from the tunnel and looked toward his companion. "They're coming to the chamber door and talking excitedly. But the peepholes carry no sound."

"Does it seem as if they may open the chamber door?" asked Tassoran edgily. He stepped away from the small tunnel and observed with satisfaction that it once more looked like solid stone.

"They're opening the chamber," Konarr said. "Ha! Now they're excited!"

"Will they sound an alarm, do you think?"

"It does not look as if they will," Konarr answered slowly, "There—one of them almost stepped into the room. I suppose he saw the slab ajar. Unfortunately the other one stopped him."

"Fine," said Tassoran.

And he ducked into the tunnel for the third time, and it reappeared the moment he touched the "surface" of the stone.

Behind him he could hear Konarr. "He sees the tunnel now—both of them do! You should be able to hear them."

Yes, thought Tassoran, *and they can hear you; wish I'd thought of that, but too late now!*

"Ho, Veneste, it *is* magic, as I said—first the slab, then the tunnel, then the voices."

It was a languid voice that came to Tassoran as he crouched waiting in the tunnel, round its corner so that he could not be seen from the door.

"Oh, very well, Hallon, it is magic. Everything here is magic. Naturally. Just don't go inside investigating without the goblet." Veneste sounded equally languid, though his voice was deeper and richer.

"Well, get it for me, then, and let's find out what is happening."

154

Tassoran almost laughed, so clearly could he visualize Veneste drawing himself up haughtily.

"*May* I remind you," Veneste said chillily, "that we are of equal rank, and that I am not to be ordered about by you?"

"Oh, devastation be visited on your pride. My Lord Veneste, most humbly I beseech you to favor me by presenting me with that goblet?"

There was silence, then a single set of footsteps, back, forth.

"Put the cup on the floor and let's get on with it," Veneste said. There was a wooden clack of the cup being set on the stone, and then a brief sliding noise.

Tassoran saw the orange fumes grow agitated in their hovering near him; then they streaked away with rare speed.

Around the corner of the tunnel, he could hear a distinct click.

"Ha!" said Veneste, and laughed. "Like magic! Now let's look into this tunnel to nowhere."

"Not so fast," said Hallon. "The Lady's orders are, only one man in the chamber at a time. You know that."

Then there were footsteps—slow, almost hesitant footsteps.

Tassoran waited until his man was well into the room, from the sound of his steps—then with a loud cry he sprang around the corner of the tunnel and confronted the young nobleman's raised sword with his own.

Taken completely aback, even though he had been prepared for the unusual, the young Hallon stood motionless for a long moment. Then he took a step backward, then two, slowly working the tip of his sword around in tiny spirals, and Tassoran admired the way he had recovered himself. Still—

"*Houl paradonalosiath vellemascabar chul tivithu* Zamaba—Zamaba—Zamaba!" Tassoran chanted.

Once more Hallon stopped in his tracks.

He stared at Tassoran for a moment, a look of mute appeal came over his face—and he dropped to the floor as if struck dead.

"The original '*amaqit* tongue! Very impressive," said Konarr, behind Tassoran. "What about the other one?"

Veneste had taken one careful step inside the chamber, at

155

the sound of the ancient 'amaqit language, and, seeing Hallon's collapse, stepped back into the guard chamber.

Tassoran started toward him, preparing to hurl the aeons-old Incantation of All Forgetting for a second time. In a moment, however, Veneste realized what he had to do and had lunged for the wooden cup.

But before he could grasp the cup, Tassoran had hurled his sword point-first at the man's chest.

The sword caught Veneste in the shoulder instead. Reacting to the pain, he tried nonetheless to stagger toward the cup, but lurched awkwardly sidewise instead, fell, and his forehead slammed into the lintel. There was one weak moan, then silence except for four men breathing, two strongly, two weakly.

"*Very* impressive," said Konarr. "Now if you will recover the Sigil of Tron, we can consider how to remove ourselves from this place."

"The Lady Tza has a certain style of economy in her magic workings," said Tassoran, taking the wooden cup and peering inside at something that rattled inside. "She transformed the sigil into gravedust fumes, and thus the sigil guarded itself!"

Konarr reached for the wooden chalice to pluck the sigil out. "Let us have a look at it!" he said—but Tassoran grabbed his wrists, a shocked look on his face.

"Not inside the chamber, man, it'll transform itself back into the gravedust fumes!"

Konarr blanched.

"Come," said Tassoran, "we must be moving away from here." He started toward the slab marking Zantain's stone tunnel.

Now it was Konarr who felt a shock of alarm. "*No!*" he said. "We mustn't trust to Zantain's paths any more! Don't ask me why—if we get away with our lives we can ask him, but let us get out of this accursed hell tower!"

Tassoran was irritated; he had planned a peaceful withdrawal and now Konarr was urging him to push their good fortune, perhaps too far—to go down through the Lady Tza's own ways and staircases through the Ebon Tower, to the ground, and across the bridge that legend said she only could tread.

156

He placed his shoulder against the open slab and urged it to its former position up against Zantain's mystic passageway. "At least she may never know how we came this way—to our deaths," he said, in bitterness tempered with a very little satisfaction.

"For a practical thief," Konarr said, grinning, "you take more stock in ancient tales than any respectable young lad of four or five in Zetri town. How do you think these fine brainless fops I studied to imitate so well, yesterday, how do you think *they* reached these chambers?"

To illustrate his meaning, he dropped to his knees beside Hallon's body, which moved slightly in its unconsciousness as Konarr touched it.

Understanding, Tassoran started searching the relaxed body of Veneste, and presently came across a small wire spiral with a regular pattern of notches in the wire.

He showed it to Konarr, who nodded and presently located a similar device on Hallon. It seemed clear that the two pieces of wire fitted together to form a complex heliform structure that had a look of being *complete* about it.

"I'll be busy holding to my incantation later," said Tassoran, "and think it best you carry this. I suspect it will protect us while we are in the tower."

Konarr nodded, and they went out into the guard chamber.

Now Tassoran reached inside the wooden goblet and took out a small carved piece of some aged, cracked wood, stained with the millennia. "Not much for the eye, certainly," he said. "The carvings seem not to make sense."

"It's not very impressive," Konarr agreed.

Tassoran put the sigil back in the cup and fitted it securely, if with some difficulty, into his leathern pouch.

Then, Tassoran in the lead and hoping he still retained the strength for another burst of the 'amaqit-chant if they should come across someone else in the Ebon Tower, they left the guard room and started down the black marble steps outside.

Nothing happened as they made their way downward except that they noticed the smell of cinnamon and mint and clove and countless other scents and fragrances eddying through the air in endless changing combinations . . .

"The Lady's gardens," muttered Konarr. "I have heard there is not their like in all the New Lands for varied rich-

157

nesses of nature . . . and they are witching scents, for certain!"

Tassoran assented, then resumed worrying how long they had before something interrupted the smooth eventlessness of their flight.

Presently, he knew.

They came to the foot of the Ebon Tower, where they were startled to see for the first time an expanse of white marble—great glittering white paves that led outside through great open arches to the vision of the gardens just beyond the moat of deadly fishes. And, beyond the endless delight of the gardens, the impressive bulk of the Lesser Palace, its windows still ablaze with light in the gloom of night—and the supreme magnificence of the Greater Palace, it's glory shrouded now. For it was still some days to the end of the fiftyday, though spring was running strong in every living thing. Come the Festival of High Spring, and the Greater Palace would be thrown open to the winter courtiers and all the great families, noble and wealthy, of Zetri, and mad revelry would split the nights asunder for long weeks after . . .

And—advancing across from the Lesser Palace was the Lady Tza, a white cloak lightly shielding her from the crisp night air, leading a full company of hawk-helmeted men— and they were within a dozen paces of the far end of the narrow footbridge over the wide, wide moat!

Konarr yelped with surprise and tossed the interlocked wire helix up in the air. The two men saw its path as a glowing arc, before it hit a white slab by the verge of the dew-moist grass, then bounced hissing and steaming into the grass.

Behind them on the stairs came footsteps, and angry shouts.

Then Konarr pointed at the narrow bridge, and his voice quavered in horror!

"There! Do you not see it! It must be a gaphalon, see, see the arms, so many of them, twenty, forty . . . we can't get by, lad! It throws its arms over the walkway itself . . ."

"Come on, old captain," Tassoran laughed, "we'll make it! See—the gaphalon has already drawn back!"

"That's thin hope for a man still in the strength of his latter youth," Konarr answered, as they started to run for the footbridge.

"Here's a better one," said Tassoran, grasping Konarr's strong right hand. "Hold on—I can see we aren't going to make it any other way. I hope I get the spell right—and don't let go, or you won't be covered!"

Tassoran muttered hastily under his breath; Konarr made no sense of the words, even when it became obvious he was repeating the same three or four words over and over again, quickly, in different patterns.

"There!" said Tassoran. "That completes the nine of nines. Hold on and we'll try to get out of here without any more of these bothersome interruptions . . . And don't talk to me—I must concentrate on repeating the magic schema . . ."

They began running again.

It was moments before Kónarr realized—concentrating as he was on the new and difficult problem of holding Tassoran's left hand as they ran—that the several dozen arms of the gaphalon that he had clearly seen thrashing wildly a moment ago were now frozen, without any motion he could see.

They were so close to the monster as they passed onto the footbridge itself, that Konarr could even see, in one wild glance, the drops of water themselves, hanging motionless in the air, suspended in their various paths from initial up to inevitable down.

But Konarr found that too much for his habits of mind, and he turned his head the other way as they reached the midpoint of the footbridge.

Deep into the otherwise placid waters of the righthand side of the moat, there extended a clear and distinct funnel of air thrusting the water aside—or so it seemed to Konarr. At the base of the funnel and almost impossible to outline, hung a gigantic shadowy shape, barely visible and that only through some strange natural phosphoresence that surrounded it.

The sight somehow was infinitely more horrible than the gaphalon, and Konarr wrenched his eyes away from . . . *whatever* lurked at the bottom of that funnel.

As they reached the other side of the bridge, they could clearly see the swarming guards frozen in their strides as they ran toward the Ebon Tower. In their forefront still was the Lady Tza herself, now only half a dozen strides from them.

Konarr shuddered in another spasm of deeper horror than any before.

For as they ran past the Lady Tza on a quartering run away from the body of men she led, he looked into her blue eyes—and *saw her eyes move*, following the two interlopers as they ran!

Then they were past and away from the mass of soldiers and the Lady, and ahead was only one more barrier—the great iron gates to the Queen's Quarter.

If the Spell of Holding continued to work long enough, they could be outside of the city of Zetri, and with a fighting chance to find a bolthole should neither Zantain nor Shagon come to their aid.

Konarr shot one look back at the lady and her men—and saw that the Lady had moved forward a stride, one single, slow, and almost meaningless step forward.

It made no difference if she were slowing down the two thieves or herself speeding up to their rate—if she increased the similarity of their rates, she could catch them—her magic would quickly undo their borrowed spells. There was no time to worry. He found the endurance to warn Tassoran of the new threat by speeding past the younger man for a moment, and indicating their rear.

Tassoran looked back—and saw the Lady complete another long slow stride. Her arms had also moved upward, were beginning an ice-river-slow gesture that could mean . . . anything, but certainly something dangerous.

Tassoran ran faster.

The spell held till they reached the main gates—then with a shock that wrenched their insides, the two men were halted in mid-stride—held fast, unable to move!

They did not need to do the now-impossible, to look back, in order to know the Lady would be up to them soon.

And they could not even speak, to offer each other so much as one man's final guesture of regret to another for friendship involuntarily cut short, or even to curse whatever they might have wished to curse . . .

There was a great bright white crackle of sound and light, and a high toneless female shriek of rage.

Immediately the two men felt themselves falling forward, released from the Lady's own Holding spell. They caught themselves, and ran forward, looking about uncertainly.

"Onto those beasts there," came a shout. "Quick, there's no

more time! I barely got these monsters here in time as it was. Run, curse you, or by the Spear of . . ."

Konarr slapped at Tassoran's shoulder, grinned weakly, gestured at a tall figure in black cloak who bestrode one of several low-to-the-ground beasts, and said only "Zantain." Then they made for the other two beasts that stood next to Zantain's.

The riding was almost too much for Konarr, as exhaustion swept over him.

He found he hadn't noticed, before climbing onto the beast, how many legs the thing had. He thought it might be six, but he could not believe that. Odd, he reflected groggily, how the mind refused to do anything to help a man sometimes. But he didn't really care.

There was now only jouncing and forgetting and slipping away into moments of unconsciousness. He had noticed glowings and flashings of fire behind them on their trail, after they'd started away on the beasts, and somebody had said that would delay 'them' a while, but it made no sense to Konarr whatever, and he wondered only about those six legs. He knew of two-legged burden-animals, and four-legged, and in the eastern lands eight-legged animals were far more common than any other, but he had never heard of a six-legged animal before, though now he was certain this one was . . .

Konarr was grateful to realize, in one last brief lucid moment before falling soundly unconscious from fatigue, that the beast's back had a natural, if somewhat bony, saddle, and that a man trained to the horse and the *arall* could doze and even sleep deeply if necessary, and then there was no need to do anything but relax and let whatever was to happen do as it wished with him, and he fell asleep.

161

CHAPTER EIGHT: *Immortal's Dawn*

KONARR was jolted awake when the three animals came to a sudden stop.

"The kephts can go no further," said Zantain. "They were not bred to run for many hours without rest or pause."

"Are we safe?" Konarr asked, groggy with the unsatisfied hunger for more sleep.

"Ha!" said Zantain, and laughed. "We are pursued closely by the Lady Tza herself and twice a hundred of her finest Hawk Guards. And by a different route Shagon trails us, by himself, and I think that he is more dangerous than she and all her men."

"Mmmm," Konarr said, his soldier's instincts rousing. He looked about in the darkness, aware that there was that slight but growing tension in the air that indicated dawn was approaching. "We must be near the Baragan Hills, by the scent of tarnflower and songleaf in the air."

"We passed the Tomb of Lord Vurda a quarter of an hour back," agreed Zantain.

"I see a low cliff over there," said Tassoran. "And I can hear the sound of running water. Perhaps we might make a kind of stand with our backs against the cliff, with Zantain's aid, for he seems a mighty worker in these hidden matters . . ."

"I think we shall make a stand here," said Zantain, "but do not look for me to save you with some gesture of the hand. Only if Shagon reaches us in time will this night end in a good clean dawn . . ."

They rode the kephts out of a wooded glade heavy with the scent and nighttime murmur of a carpet of songleaf herb, till they came to a shallow, swift-running stream, perhaps twice or thrice wider than a tall man's stride.

Beyond the brook was a patch of low, grassy land. Directly behind that stood a low cliff that fronted the stream as far up and down it as they could see, save for the half-acre or so of grass in front of them.

The kephts splashed ponderously through the stream and clambered exhaustedly up a low bank on the far side, and the three men slid off their mounts.

Silently Konarr and Tassoran looked to Zantain to speak or act, that they might follow. The two needed the exchange of only one glance to agree that here was a man who *knew* what he was doing. They were both grateful for the removal, at last, of the burdens of unaccustomed heights of responsibility.

Their mood was broken almost immediately, by a low distant roll of thunder reverberating over the plains from Zetri to the Baragan Hills in an ominous overture.

"Not a cloud in the starry sky," whispered Tassoran, looking upward in awe.

The thunder died away, then began again, louder—nearer.

There was a crackle, and a gigantic stroke of lightning slammed into the top of the cliff behind them, toppling several small boulders over the verge to come crashing down onto their grassy haven.

"He is almost upon us," observed Zantain calmly. "You might draw your swords, my comrades. It will not deter him. But he had a certain admiration for bravery once."

Tassoran looked doubtful, but Konarr laughed aloud and drew his sword with a flourish.

"Weapons are useless!"

The rolling of distant thunder and the echo of the clap at the clifftop died away suddenly.

The strange new voice boomed over the grassy patch between cliff and stream.

"I want only the Sigil of Tron. Give me it, and you shall depart in peace."

The strange voice died away, and they looked about.

Presently Tassoran pointed to the top of the cliff. "Shagon," he said to the other two.

Zantain shook his head. "That is not anyone called Shagon," he said, and was interrupted by the voice.

"I am Shagon," it said. *"But Shagon is Azeltarem. As you*

163

know that, you must now die. Unfortunate. I would have kept my word and let you leave in peace."

Konarr and Tassoran looked as one toward Zantain.

Zantain stood wrapped in black, only his strong face visible. On it was a smile, a smile which broadened as they watched.

Then in the distance Konarr heard the sound of a horn. He recognized it—a scout, signaling their trail back to the main body of men accompanying the Lady Tza. Doubtless she would be here in minutes. The thought did not cheer him, nor, when he glanced at Tassoran, did the lad seem entirely contented . . .

But Zantain laughed and clapped the two of them on the shoulder. "Stalemate at least," he said, the first word in a tongue unknown to them—which caused Tassoran to start with alarm.

Zantain looked upward to the top of the cliff, perhaps three stories above them. Shagon—or Azeltarem—had stepped to the verge and was now clearly visible to those below.

It was clear the Black Magician's attention had been suddenly drawn elsewhere.

"See," Zantain said, "how he feels the presence of another power whose vastnesses resemble his own. The Lady approaches!"

There was a growing thunder of hoofs, almost loud enough to rival the mutter of the heavens at Azeltarem's approach.

Then, across the stream, appeared a body of half a dozen horsemen, who drew back immediately upon realizing they had run their quarry to ground. The horses pawed the damp grassy earth, snorting and slavering with their recent exertions, and upset by the presence of the kephts.

Konarr became aware of a chanting from the top of the cliff—Azeltarem preparing some new hell's work, he realized. But there was no time to wonder. Across the stream now there was a flash of streaming white through the trees, and then the Lady Tza herself at the head of a large troop of Hawk Guards.

"*Stop!*" came the Lady's clear strong voice, and Azeltarem halted in the midst of his incantation.

"*Very well,*" said Azeltarem in a cold hard voice, dry as autumn in the last chill before snows fall heavily. "*It seems *your power was as reported to me—dangerously close to my own. It will now be necessary to take other actions."*

The Lady's laughter rang sharply over the innocent splashing of the stream—for, Konarr brooded, only the natural things of the Baragan Hills dared speak when two such adversaries met each other.

"You are too gross to harm me," said the Lady, *"and you burn with conflicting desires, old hellworker. I think my affairs will proceed substantially as I have planned them, as soon as these fools here are wrecked and destroyed and the Sigil of Tron once more in my power to use as I see fit!"*

"Try," said Zantain.

Konarr blinked and Tassoran shook his head, realizing he had understood nothing that had been said.

"You . . . man," said Tza slowly in a new low voice, speaking the word "man" as if it were not so much unpleasant as an irrelevancy. *"You dare to dare my powers? You shall suffer!"*

The Lady's mount stepped nervously about in a half circle and she soothed it with a whispered phrase till it was calm again. Then, as casually as if she were tossing a shuttlecock or a child's innocent toy, she gestured in a throwing motion toward Zantain, who stood impassive.

A sheet of flame as thick as a man's body poured from the Lady's hand toward Zantain—but with a casual gesture of his own hand, the flame seemed to stop at the very surface of his skin, harming him no more than the chill night air might.

For a long moment the Lady Tza held her hand motionless, pointing toward Zantain, and the sheet of flame poured forth upon him, and he smiled as he had smiled before, unconcernedly.

Konarr felt she looked quite uncertain for the first time.

"Very well," she said. *"Then I—"*

"One moment," said Azeltarem quietly from the low cliff-top. *"I too admit that I should like that sigil for my uses, good lady. So . . ."*

Azeltarem uttered a single word in an unknown tongue, and his hands gestured in the air.

In a moment, there stood a pillar of . . . blackness, taller and bulkier than the figure of a man, hanging in the air in front of Azeltarem.

165

Hanging over Zantain's head—and then descending.

The Lady Tza studied the figure of the man as he stood up as impassively to the shape of nightmare black as to her own torrents of white-hot flame.

The blackness enveloped Zantain . . .

. . . and dissolved away in the breeze.

"So," Azeltarem cried angrily, *"you are indeed that danger I have been awaiting. It is good to know one's enemy—just as, my Lady, it is good at last to see one's enemy. There are many new things now to occur . . ."*

Azeltarem's voice grew louder as he addressed the white-clad woman across the stream. *"But as for now, let us, you and I, bend our powers and efforts together in a force that shall destroy this stranger to our affairs, who has cast our present projects into confusion."*

Zantain turned to face the Lady Tza, an ironic smile on his face. "You know that now to be impossible, do you not?"

"Yes," she answered. *"But to join forces with . . . him . . ."*

"You pause to think too much, Madame Queen," said Zantain. "Tassoran, your pouch—give me the wooden cup."

Tassoran fumbled at the knotted strands of leather that held the pouch securely shut.

"No!" thundered Azeltarem, and his voice was swept away in a mad raging thunder twice as loud as that before. A black flash of lightning blasted into the streambank directly beside Zantain, causing the water of the stream to flicker for a moment with a sickening dark glow, and searing the grass for yards around him.

Tassoran gulped and blessed his hasty knots for delaying him—perhaps this Zantain could take such a bolt, but not he. "There never was such thing as an invulnerable thief before," he said aloud. without realizing he was speaking.

And Konarr grinned.

"The cup," said Zantain calmly, and strode toward Tassoran, who quickly drew his knife, sliced the knotted thongs, and took out the wooden cup, the wooden sigil rattling inside.

Hastily Tassoran passed the cup to Zantain and stepped back away from him.

There was a freshening of breeze, bearing grass scents, and then, without warning, they were being battered by a high

166

wind, keening through the branches of the trees and whipping about them frantically.

And above it they heard the mighty thundering voice of Azeltarem. Arms spread over his head, his fingers spat tiny black lightnings, while about him the whipping winds lashed furiously out at everything.

"Winds, winds, winds, rise, sweep, destroy, crack the trees and shatter the mountains, at my command rise, rise, break these mortals back to mud and slime, crush, batter, blow, winds, rise, rise, rise—destroy!"

Tassoran fell to his knees at the force of the wind, then threw himself full-length to keep from being swept away.

Konarr planted one knee firmly on the ground, braced himself, and continued to observe the scene as best he could.

Across the stream he saw the Lady Tza, her face clouded with anger, her lips moving to some enchantment of her own, as she tried to keep her men together and protected from the mad cyclonic winds.

And Zantain reached into the wooden cup, drew out the wooden Sigil of Tron, and raised it high in both his hands.

Azeltarem's thunderous chant fell silent, and the Lady Tza stopped in the middle of a phrase to stare at Zantain's hands.

In one moment there was ultimately ferocious wind.

In the next, silence. Peace.

Not a person moved, nor a breath of wind, nor was there any kind of sound except for the subdued nickering of the Lady's horse, upset by the violence of the wind before and the even more shattering quiet now.

No, Konarr realized, everything was *not* silent, after all. Small insects chirred in the grass, and there were bird songs from the forest.

Dawn approached, and the forest seemed undisturbed by the brutality of the enchanted wind.

Dawn . . . no, Konarr realized again, the light was not the light of dawn.

Held high in his two hands over Zantain's head, the Sigil of Tron glowed ever brighter and brighter with a pure dazzling sunshine light, bathing the glade, the stream, the cliff, the forest, and all those assembled with a midday blaze.

Then the glow in Zantain's hands became so bright no eyes could hold on it, and all looked away, seeing their surround-

167

ings ever more and more brightened by the ever more and more impossible blast of pure light energy emanating from the sigil.

Then, at an impossible peak of brilliance, the light winked out.

They rubbed their eyes and tried to see clearly again in the dimness, now lifted somewhat by the growing light of the true and rising sun.

Zantain's hands were empty.

An inarticulate howl of rage came from Azeltarem, and he started once more to gesture, while the Lady Tza said nothing—but her lips were moving again.

"Enough!" said Zantain with a gesture. "I have absorbed the power of the sigil; it is mine now. This game is done and I have won, for now."

He did not seem to speak loudly, but Konarr felt the new strength in the man. Zantain stood even taller and straighter, poised and charged with energy. His voice rang with calm assurance.

And Azeltarem uttered a syllable of disgust, started to make a gesture, shook his head with another sound of disgust —and vanished.

Konarr turned to look at the Lady Tza.

Already her men were turning their horses and heading silently and slowly back the way they had come, back to Zetri.

But the Lady Tza stayed at the same spot till the last of her men had left the glade at the far side of the stream, staring over at Zantain.

And Zantain had turned to his kepht, and was gently leading it over to the stream for water. A moment later, Konarr, followed immediately by Tassoran, did the same.

So for a time the three kephts drank deeply and noisily from the splashing stream, while silent hawk-helmeted guardsmen rode stiffly away, and while the silent figure of the Lady Tza sat quietly mounted on her horse, still staring over at Zantain.

As the last hawk-helmet disappeared into the forest, she started a trifle, leaned over, patted her horse on the head, whispered to it, turned its head with the reins, and herself rode away, still in silence.

The three men did not speak for some time after her departure . . .

"Explanations?" said Zantain suddenly, with a chuckle, and taking the other two by surprise. "Explanations are tedious. But you deserve a few. Sit you down and examine the packs on your mounts. There is food and drink for all of us, and bedding. I propose we sleep through the morning, and ride this afternoon."

The two men fell upon the food ravenously.

"The Lady Tza and Azeltarem," Zantain continued, while they ate, "are, as you know, evils opposite to each other. There are only the two, for there are no mothers and daughters successive to the Lady—she is herself, now exactly as she was a thousand, perhaps two thousand, or three or four thousand years ago. You must pardon some vagueness; I have come from a long rest and all is not yet clear to me.

"Azeltarem is older, far older—may go back to the Old Lands themselves . . . These two search for power, that is clear. And there are many elder talismans, cast into the New Lands along with those few people who survived the doom of Pazatar and Armassic."

Zantain paused, and ran a hand over his face, a troubled look shadowing his confident manner. "Pazatar and . . . Armassic. But I do not remember . . ."

Konarr blinked at Zantain's halt and puzzlement. The man seemed so powerful, so certain of himself. He had withstood the ultimate tests of the mightiest workers of magic in all the New Lands, and spoke of unveiling old mysteries as casually as if he himself had helped draw the veils over them.

"It is not important at this time," Zantain said, visibly pulling his attention back from wandering. "All will be made clear in time; that is the promise.

"For now, it is only clear that these two dark masters Azeltarem and Tza can partly foresee the future. Our fortune lies in that, since all they saw was some strange interrupting foreshadowing their deep endeavors. I know, for I too have this power from time to time. When I decided to awaken from my rest as a simple old innkeeper, it was only because I had noticed portents myself—because Azeltarem and Tza, foreseeing me, took blind actions that awoke my sleeping attention!"

Konarr frowned; Tassoran spoke for the first time. "Most marvelously circular, friend. No doubt it is the way of magical affairs, which is why I never cared for such. But how did I, and old captain here, come to be a part of such high mysterious matters?"

"Seeing inexplicable difficulties arising in the path of his attempt to gain the Sigil of Tron from the Ebon Tower, where the Lady Tza held it in preparation for her fateful onslaughts—now forestalled—Azeltarem wanted aid. As Shagon, an old device of his, he looked for a highly skilled professional thief, and found one, hiring him by destroying the grown devlet set on his trail by his elder brother, a devious Spellmaster of Sezain called Taher Kmatis . . . If Azeltarem had not found you, however," Zantain said to Tassoran, "he would merely have searched the Thieves' Quarter in Zetri; finding you was chance."

The two men kept silence.

Zantain continued. "As I watched the two of you fight, I saw in you a crux of the coming conflict. Shagon was going to take one of you, clearly; and I suspected who he was. But I was far too weak yet; I needed one to act for me. Hence Konarr, acting for me even to the extent of finding his way through my own shadow tunnels!"

He smiled, then laughed. "There, that should be complex enough to satisfy your thirsts for now! The time has come for more direct proposals, firstly this: follow me, and if you live you shall know all. Decline, and I say no more."

"I will follow you," said Tassoran suddenly. "I do not need to hear your 'secondly.' "

Konarr blinked with surprise, then grunted with irritation and said, grumbling, "I too."

But Tassoran went on as if he had not heard.

"Zantain . . ." Tassoran mused. "It comes to me that name is familiar in an old Kazemi legend, and it is not a common name—though I have heard of mothers taking it for their sons . . . yes, I will follow!"

Zantain nodded. "Do you know the legends of the Vanished Ones?"

Half in the singsong fashion of the legend-hawking storytellers in every marketplace of the New Lands, Tassoran responded.

170

"The Vanished Ones—the High Gods! Lord Tir'u of All the Waters, and his Lady Oriada slain with a skybolt hurled by Limnar, from the high peak of Mount Yarnath which is of Tormitan. And Sleepless Touraj, the heir of Vahith and Yarthob, awaits in the silence, in blind darkness; Guardian of the Horn of Althar, uncaring he awaits in blind darkness. Uncaring he awaits his doom or glory! Touraj the Guardian, in the Hidden Place! The Madnesses of TIRBADA under the Swamps, and the—"

Konarr broke in. "Tales for children. The gods, if such there be, have not trod common dirt since the Old Lands foundered."

"Pazatar and Armassic," said Zantain, quietly and with great assurance, "did *not* founder and sink into the waves, as many think. The Old Lands to this day lie open to the warm sun and the clean fresh air. But only silence reigns. No man speaks or acts there. And as the Old Lands are still real, so the High Gods are still real, and their relics—as, the Sigil of Tron. These latter are great prizes, and—"

Konarr clenched his fists and tried to control his anger. "Would you have us storm Yarnath and the God Lands? Why do you tell us of Mysteries common men like us should never know? Or do you, perhaps, but test us for some secret purpose, as being secretly the creature of the Lady, or perhaps Azeltarem himself?"

Zantain uncorked a leathern flask and drank deeply from it. Then he offered it, first to Konarr, who shook his head in angry 'no,' then to Tassoran, who drank deeply and with gusto.

"Test you?" said Zantain. "Yes. For my own purposes, however, and not for those of the ominous Lady, nor for the subtle Azeltarem. So far you have proven worthy. Because of that, I shall draw my sword."

Once more Konarr shook his head in helpless irritation and anger, as Zantain unslung his great cudgel from behind the kepht's natural saddle. As old Durrekal's, that cudgel was as familiar to Konarr as the inn named after it.

Puzzled, Konarr watched while Zantain, smiling slightly, brandished the club in the air a moment.

Then Konarr blinked indeed. This strange man called Zantain now held a golden-hilted long-sword in his right hand,

and an empty dagger case at his waist had become a long, richly-figured leathern scabbard.

"There is much I still have to remember," said Zantain. "I am not yet fully sure what year this is that I have returned to awareness in, nor do I really know what has transpired in so long a period. I do not even well remember my life as Vesalye.

"So I cannot tell you whether this sword of mine has remained sheathed in its battered, rustic disguise for a thousand or for ten thousand years.

"This sword is Legend. 'Tis said its blade is made of a magic alloy of diamond and silver."

And Zantain brandished the glittering blade in the sparkling dawnlight; for the sun was over the horizon and the Baragan Hills, pouring his fresh warm strength over the hills and the plains, over the cities of the righteous and wicked, and throughout the New Lands from Ank and Oan by the Sea of Cheg to the western shores of Tarmisorn . . .

Konarr whispered in awe, "As a child in Kolkorth I had heard tales of such a blade, held by a nameless hero of the Old Lands themselves."

"Not nameless," said Tassoran in a low voice shaking with awe. "They called him Zantain—the Longlived."

Zantain sheathed his sword.

"No," he said. "I am Zantain—the Immortal. And if you join me for the battles yet to come, another tale begins this very dawn!"

They looked at him, neither able to speak.

But Zantain turned away from them, looking over the stream and the copse of trees on the other side, looking from the Baragan Hills over the plains of Tarmisorn.

"There are two more to be found," he said, in a low voice. "I wonder where they are, who they are. And I wonder when we shall find them."

He looked back at the two men; there was no need to ask if they would follow now.

Zantain smiled as the breezes whipped his cloak about him.

"Then we are three—three of the Five Heroes of a new game, a new tale, a new romance!"

He laughed aloud, and jumped onto his kepht. Then Tassoran laughed and did the same, and finally Konarr, caught up in the spirit at last, mounted his own.

"Do men sleep at the start of a new age?" said Zantain, almost shouting. "Do we lie abed at the dawn of such a day?"

He roused the kepht, which grunted and began to move forward. "Ride with me!"

And, talking and laughing all together, the three men rode across the stream and into the trees, and were gone from sight.

THE END

173

FLYING SAUCERS

The only new approach
to the mystery of UFOs

FLYING SAUCERS
ARE WATCHING US

by Otto O. Binder
renowned space expert

A startling theory, scientifically docu-
mented, that details **why** flying saucers
are here, and why they have been observing us for centuries. **This is not a report of
sightings, or a discussion of whether or not
UFOs exist.** It is the "why" of the world's
greatest mystery.

FREE BOOKS!

Choose any 4 exciting Belmont Books listed below and receive the fifth book absolutely free! Choose 7 books and get 2 additional books free!

☐ **THE LIVING DEMONS,** by Robert Bloch
Monstrous creatures swarm beyond the boundaries of their nightmare world.
#B50-787, 50¢

☐ **TIME UNTAMED,** anthology
★8★ amazing science fiction tales first time in paperback by all time greats—
Isaac Asimov, Robert Bloch, Ray Bradbury, Clifford D. Simak, John Wyndham,
Theodore Sturgeon, L. Sprague de Camp, and Fritz Leiber.   #B50-781, 50¢

☐ **SPECIAL DELIVERY / STAR GLADIATOR,** by Kris Neville / Dave Van Arnam
Two alien races battle for an unwary earth . . . How long can a lone man
survive the brutality of 50 worlds? Two complete full length novels. #B50-788, 50¢

☐ **AFTER SOME TOMORROW,** by Mack Reynolds
A world could be changed by ESP, but only if a man wanted to risk everything.
#B50-795, 50¢

☐ **THE COUNTERFEITS,** by Leo F. Kelley
It was business as usual on earth and no one suspected the sky held something
more than the sun, the moon and the stars.   #B50-797, 50¢

☐ **TOWER AT THE EDGE OF TIME,** by Lin Carter
What strange powers thrust the warrior and two men of greed into the limbo
beyond time?   #B50-804, 50¢

☐ **THE THIEF OF THOTH,** by Lin Carter
Does crime pay—if a galaxy is the prize?
AND OTHERS SHALL BE BORN, by Frank Belknap Long
Not quite human . . . not quite alien—but inexplicably dangerous.   #B50-809, 50¢

☐ **ASYLUM EARTH,** by Bruce Elliot
The unseen but deadly battle between the world of no time and no place . . .
and the here and now of Earth.   #B50-819, 50¢

☐ **THE NON-STATISTICAL MAN,** by Raymond F. Jones
One man's mind spins a taut and eerie arc from the dark past into the distant
future and suddenly the world looks different.   #B50-820, 50¢

☐ **EARTH UNAWARE,** by Mack Reynolds
His unearthly power could destroy the world—was there no one to stop him?
#B50-826, 50¢

NON-FICTION

☐ **WORLD OF THE WEIRD,** by Brad Steiger
Startling, astounding, shocking . . . but incredibly true! A collection of stories
of human beings, and animals who defy all known laws of science and nature.
#B50-727, 50¢

☐ **FINDERS KEEPERS,** by Warren Smith
YOU can find millions in lost and buried treasure! Here are the inside tips on
how to locate money, gold and jewels for yourself!   #B60-061, 60¢

☐ **ADVENTURES IN TOMORROW,** by Kendell Foster Crossen
Isaac Asimov, A. E. Van Vogt, Ray Bradbury, Theodore Sturgeon, Anthony
Boucher, Forrest J. Ackerman, Bruce Elliot and 9 more of the world's greatest
science fiction authors.   #B75-215, 75¢

☐ **A PAIR FROM SPACE,** by James Blish and Robert Silverberg
First paperback publication of two major science fiction novels—complete.
#B92-612, 50¢

☐ **A LAMP FOR MEDUSA,** by William Tenn
THE PLAYERS OF HELL, by Dave Van Arnam
First paperback publication of Tenn's classic novel—plus a tense novel by a new
master of swords and sorcery. SF.   #B60-077, 60¢

☐ **FLYING SAUCERS ARE WATCHING US,** by Otto O. Binder
New evidence and startling scientific finds lead to a startling answer to the UFO
riddle.   #B75-218, 75¢
